Tempted to Touch

Nigeria Lockley

Inheritance Books
P.O. Box 451
New York, New York 10030

For anyone who has ever been tempted.

Acknowledgements

Abba Father, I thank you for watching over me and providing me with the help I needed for this journey.

Myriam Skye Holly, you are my champion, my friend, my critique partner, and my cover girl. Thank you for lending me everything good that God has placed inside of you.

Thank you, Michelle Stimpson, for giving me advice on writing in the first person and praying with me when the rest of my life looked like a first draft.

NoNo, you started this madness and encouraged me to step out of my comfort zone and listen to the voice of my character. Thank you for the push. Thank you for your friendship. I love you, sissy.

Thank you to my beta readers: LaVern Perscell, Sharon Blount, Tamara Young, and Teresa Beasley, for taking time to read Tempted to Touch in its early stages and provide me with feedback.

Michelle Chester, thank you once again for editing my work while still allowing me to maintain my dignity. I love you for that.

I want to extend a special thank you to Trishannah Amuquandoh for sharing her story with me. When I began writing the character Nate and I realized he had some challenges I wondered how I was going to find time to conduct the research, but the very next day Trishannah walked into my class and just shared her story with me. For that I am forever grateful.

Finally, thank you to each and every person who purchased Tempted to Touch. This book is special to me because it is the first book published by Inheritance Books. Thank you for sowing into my dream and I pray that you are blessed by this book. Welcome to the family.

Watch and pray, that ye enter not into temptation: the spirit indeed is willing,

but the flesh is weak."

Matthew 26:41

Chapter 1

"Do you remember that Gospel Choir Ensemble contest, Songs of Zion that I entered?" my husband, Mason, asked as he walked up the steps of our two-family home. A wide grin decorated his bearded face exposing his gap teeth. The title of the contest sounded familiar, but I couldn't recall it. Mason was always on a mission or expedition in the name of the Lord.

Mason zoomed through the house like a tidal wave landing right in front of me and washed my face with kisses.

"Stop it, Mason. Stop," I said, sliding my face away from his sticky, wet lips. "What is going on?" I asked even though I knew what was coming—*God is good, and He's expanding my territory* and a few other traditional celebratory remarks. My husband said those kinds of things when he was worked up. I have to admit that I was curious about where the sudden injection of delight came from to have him bouncing off the walls. Boys in the Hood, the non-profit he worked for, drained all of his energy. It wasn't easy keeping young men off the streets and out of jail, but he tried. The only time he was this excited was when something "amazing" had transpired at our church, New Visions of Christ, where he served as minister of music, or one of his boys had gotten their GED or beat a case. Nor did Mason make it home before nine o'clock unless it was his turn to pick up our son, Nathan, from school.

"Spit it out, Mase," I demanded, tapping the desk in my makeshift office. "What's going on? You're only this excited when one of your boys beats a case or a new member joins New Visions. Which one is it today?"

"You're not going to believe this." He paused and gathered two bunches of his thick, jet black locs and folded them behind his head. A few loose strands hung off his shoulders.

"Come on with it, Mr. Seagram. I was doing something before you barged in here."

"Work or pleasure? You work too hard." He tapped my nose with the tip of his finger. "I'd like to spend a little more time with you."

"A bit of both," I responded with a smile. "I'm doing the kind of work that pleases me." *I hope you'll respect that*, I wanted to add, but I didn't feel like exploring any of Mason's issues with my love for my job or pre- occupation with worldly affairs. Mason should know that it was rare for me to detach myself from the goings-on of the household to retreat into this pocket of a room. When we moved into this house eight years ago it was difficult for us to find suitable tenants to rent the top floor out to. Our plan had been to rent the top floor and use the proceeds to pay for some of our son, Nate's, extensive medical bills. We realized we needed the cash after the newborn screening during my pregnancy revealed that Nate had inherited the sickle cell hemoglobin. A second blood test was performed, and it showed that he wasn't as lucky as I was to just carry the trait. The doctors diagnosed him with full blown sickle cell anemia while still in the womb. Since the top floor was vacant Mason took it over and turned it into a study and prayer room while I got stuck in a linen closet with pasty yellow walls for an office.

"I can't take the suspense," I said, running my tongue along my teeth. I tugged at the bottom of his white and navy blue striped polo shirt guiding him to the folding chair near my desk. His enthusiasm didn't faze me, but once he settled down and stopped bouncing off the tiles his stillness drew me in. Even though Mason is only 5'8" he filled a space with his presence. His round, brown eyes and dangerously long lashes demanded my attention before his story trickled out of his full lips.

"What are you doing?" he asked, peering over my shoulder avoiding the chair. The high he had when he came in must have worn off because he slipped back into his usual unaffectionate self.

"I was feeling creative, so I sat down to write a song or two once Nate got settled."

"Good." He smiled. "The choir needs new praise and worship songs," he announced, eyeing my notebook.

I tilted my head up towards him. "Would you like me to sing a little for you? I promise you'll enjoy it," I moaned, puckering up my lips for a kiss. Mason skipped my lips and pecked my head so softly he barely touched my pores. In an instant he was back to being about his Father's business. My endeavors and my desire would need to take a ride in the backseat again. Someone needed to remind Mason that the marriage bed is undefiled.

"It would be great if some of those songs you're working on were for the Lord especially since one of the producers of Sounds of Zion called me today. New Vision made it to the next round. We're going to record a song in an actual recording studio." Mason swayed side to side, the locs that were loose swung in the air behind him. His smile enlarged and spread across his round face. The euphoric feeling that controlled him when he'd entered the house had returned. Too bad I was about to crush it.

"Mase, how many times do we have to go over this? I don't want to be a gospel singer. *" I want what you promised me when we met.* That's what I wanted to say, but I was in no mood for him to remind me that only the devil dwells in the past—God is in the creating business.

"If you're searching for fame, then you really should give your gift to the Lord." I blew my lips at him expelling a short burst of air and directed my attention back on my creative endeavors. Despite my disregard he continued his impromptu sermon. "Babe," he said, stroking his beard. "Look at the widow and her mite. One coin put her into the archives of faith."

I glanced at him over my shoulder. His eyes were glistening and wet with the sparkle and dew that filled his eyes on Sunday just before he entered the pulpit to lead devotion.

"I doubt that if I write one gospel song the Lord is going to commission a new Bible just to include me."

A hearty chuckle rolled out of his mouth. Mason placed both of his hands on my shoulders and massaged them. "Your story will be written in glory. Can you imagine the procession in heaven as the Lord shows you the souls that were saved and those that returned to Him after hearing just one of your songs?"

I tilted my head backwards and I drunk in his face. Mason's eyes blinked rapidly and his smile was so wide I could see the gaping hole in the back of his mouth where his tooth had been extracted. Mason was no longer standing in the linen closet with fading wallpaper. He couldn't feel the small computer hutch we'd scored from a flea market wobbling under the pressure of our weight. He was on his way to the third heaven already. I wished I could see that clearly.

"Sounds good," I said, clearing my throat. I didn't want to rain on his parade I wanted to come down on him like a typhoon. "I'm looking for something more immediate."

"Let's say you write a good song, Pooka." He stooped over me and anointed my forehead with a kiss. "I mean a really good song; what's the most you can get?"

I shrugged my shoulders unsure of the specifics. However, I knew it was more than enough to take care of our worries and at least get me a trip to Hawaii.

"Daniel 12:3 says that those who lead the many to righteousness will shine like stars forever and ever. Oh." He shuddered. "I can't even imagine you shining like a star, Pooka."

"I can't either," I said, ducking away from the oppression of his rock head.

"What's the matter?"

"I can't see what you see." He twisted his face up as if I said something crazy. "Sorry, but I'm not super spiritual like you."

"I don't consider myself to be super spiritual."

"Of course not." I laughed. "You probably never realized that when you say grace you start speaking in tongues."

"I do not." He blushed and pinched the top of my arm.

"You do, but somehow I deal with it. Do you think you can deal with me?"

"Forever and always," he said, kissing my forehead again. "Just pray on it and God will help you to see things the way I do."

I wondered what would happen if I couldn't.

Chapter 2

My contempt for my husband and his blessed life theory stalled my creativity and kept me up much later than I wished. If it had not been for Nate hovering over my side of the bed with the grease and a comb and brush in his hand I'd still be sleeping.

"Mase, why is your son standing over me like Jason Voorhees?" I groaned into my husband's ear. Mason glared at me through one open eye, rolled over, and resumed his snoring campaign.

"Ma," Nathan whined. "I'm going to be late for school." He extended his arms towards me pushing the hair products into my face.

"Sit down." I pointed to the floor beside my bed.

Nate plopped onto the ground. I took a deep breath and prepared myself for the daunting task of combing out Nate's coarse hair until he no longer resembled a baby bison. My hope had been that his father would encourage him to cut it. But ever since Mayor De Blasio's took the stage with his son, Dante, sporting an afro that took up most of the camera, not one of my men gave in to my petition. It didn't seem to matter that this child's head had become a haven for every piece of dust in Harlem.

"You know I could braid this." I shook a corner of his hair I had gathered in my hands. "That would easily put an end to this torture."

"Ma," Nate called out.

"Leave the boy alone. Just…" Mason's words seeped out in scattered bursts still cloaked in the heaviness of sleep. "Just…let the boy do what he wants with his hair." I realigned myself so I could get a good view of Mason as he adjusted the white linen cloth that held his lengthy locs in a delicate mound that sat atop of his head. He looked better than a platter of chicken and waffles. Desire filled my belly. I wanted to scoop him up, but lately he'd been resistant to my touch. I didn't know if the chasm between us existed because we weren't in sync physically anymore or because we were not on the same level spiritually. Because of that gap, the level of intimacy necessary to sustain our marriage was depleting. Small things became big things, namely this child's head.

"You really think this is a good idea," I said, pushing back.

"Yes." He stretched across the bed and slapped a kiss on my cheek marking the end of the conversation.

Our vision and understanding of the world had become so different that I hoped his response was coming from a purely naïve place. It may be perfectly acceptable for him to walk around looking like a ragamuffin when he felt like it. I mean the rugged look was sexy on him. I'd spotted more than a couple of sisters at New Visions salivating in the sanctuary when their eyes were supposed to be closed. That look worked for him. Now, for a child traveling from Harlem to one of the most prestigious schools in the city on the Upper West Side, Emblem Prepatory Academy, a wild and unmanageable afro did not read the same.

"Ma, are we finished?" Nate asked, tugging at my pink satin pant leg of my pajamas. The ring of his prepubescent voice reeled me back into the morning focus—get him to school and get myself to work.

"Not quite," I replied, grabbing the last bushel of uncombed hair on Nate's head and raking the comb through it before sending him off to finish getting dressed. "Make it happen, I'll be ready in two minutes, Nate."

"You sure?" Nate and Mason asked in unison.

"Yes." I already had an outfit in mind, a sleek black sheath dress with a jeweled neckline. I took a quick military shower. Next I slipped into my dress, stepped into my pumps, and blew a kiss to Mason who'd finally risen from the bed and entered the bathroom to prepare for his day.

Preparation for my day officially began when I entered Harvey's House of Java, which was just a few feet away from Nate's school. After securing a thirty-two ounce cup of coffee I pushed Nate towards the exit. We moved in such a flurry there was no time for me to brace myself for a collision with another parent during the morning Manhattan shuffle. The Manhattan shuffle was what I had dubbed the mad dash from the subway into the school and out the door followed by a nod and wave at the principal, then you hurtle back through the door desperately trying to avoid the president of the PTA who was trying to corner you for your signature, a donation, or cupcakes.

I shook my head and refocused my eyes on the hand that once safely cradled my cup of Joe, which was now dripping from my fingertips and rolling up the sleeve of my trench coat.

"Are you okay, Ma?" Nate inquired, looking up at me.

"I'm sorry, Kira," a familiar voice said with his head bent in my direction and his hand full of tissues extended towards me.

"Ma, are you okay?" Nate asked again tugging on the strap of my suede tan hobo. *No, I'm stuck on stupid.* Thankfully that didn't come out of my mouth. I replied with a strong and soothing, "Yes. Hun, I'm fine," before snatching the napkins from the palm of Quincy McAdams.

"Thank you, Quincy." I dabbed at my arm and Nate pulled on my purse string again.

"Uh...who is this?" Nate asked doing his best imitation of his father's gruff voice.

"Nathan, this is Mr. McAdams, an old friend of mine," I said doing my best to appear pleasant and mask the nature of our relationship.

Quincy hiked up the legs of his tailored slate grey trousers and crouched down to Nate's height. "Nice to meet you, Nathan." He extended a balled up fist for Nate to tap. "You know," he drew back the sleeve of his blazer and glanced at his watch, "in about two minutes you will officially be marked late and I would hate for that to happen."

Nate winced. "Me too." He looked back at me. "If you're good, Mom I'm going inside," Nate declared, releasing my purse string and trotting towards the doors of Emblem Academy.

"Nate," I called to him following him out the coffee shop.

Nate turned back, smiled at me, and waved. "Bye, Ma."

Please don't leave me alone with six feet of fineness who was, by the looks of it, a lil' bit too delighted to have spilled my coffee. I waved back trying to see past the face in front of me. *Emblem Academy was a few feet away from Joe's House of Java, but I wasn't worried about Nate's safety, I was concerned about my own.* I wanted to look away from his monsoon-deep eyes, but I was too dazzled to turn away. Quincy didn't waste a moment seizing upon my apparent weakness; he inched closer as I backed away.

"Kira, if you keep backing up you're going to crash into another person. Stop playing." He grabbed the underside of the sleeve on my coat pulling me in closer. "I'm not going to bite you. I just wanted to wipe the coffee off your arm before I hug you."

I rolled my eyes and smiled. "Of all the coffee shops on the Upper West Side you could have walked into and accosted a woman in, why'd you have to walk into mine? Oh forget it." I waved my hand at him putting his response on pause. "I don't have time for your silver tongue. I have to get to work."

"My daughter attends Emblem Prep as well and today is my day to drop her off. Where do you work?"

"I'm the director of Human Resources at Cloud Nine."

"Cloud Nine." His lips curled up like he was disgusted. *It could be worse,* I thought. I know plenty of people we went to college with who were working at JC Penney right on 34th street. Don't get me wrong, there's nothing wrong with working in customer service, but you don't need a BA to ring up towels.

"Yes, Cloud Nine; one of the highest grossing cable television networks today. I'm sure you've heard of it."

"I have." He stuck his hands into his pocket "But I've always pictured you doing something different. From what I recall, you were well on your way to becoming an R&B superstar."

"Hummmph…" He remembered that. I wondered if he remembered me catching him with that freshman in the library. "Well, life led me in a different direction. What about you? Don't you have somewhere to be, like a laboratory or something?"

"Actually, I'm headed to a business meeting downtown. You want a ride?"

"No."

"Are you still mad at me? I promise you no one has ever occupied the same space in my heart that you have," he said as smooth as whip cream. Like we were the only two on the pavement.

"Good bye, Quincy." I pivoted on my heels and he followed suit demolishing any sense of personal space that I could claim to have on a sidewalk in New York City. He pulled up behind me.

"Take my card." He stuck his hand out in front of me and whispered into my ear. "If you ever get tired of life leading you and decide you want to lead your life, I'll help you out."

The embossed letters on his card read *Quincy McAdams CEO of MacMusic*. I leaned back and my head grazed his chest. I had to get out of this position. We were too close to the school for us to be this comfortable. I pulled the card out of his hand and spun around like I was a contestant on *Dancing with the Stars*. "What is this?"

"My card. If you can still sing like a skylark then I'm willing to work with you. At the bare minimum, I'll help you cut a demo or let you sing background on one of my artist's tracks." He withdrew his keys from his pocket and pressed a button. The lights on a Range Rover a few spaces ahead of us blinked. "You sure you don't want a ride."

"I'm positive, but I have your card—I'll call you when I need one."

Chapter 3

"Is that...?" Onyjie gasped after flipping my laptop open as I tried to press it closed when she entered my office.

"Yes, that's Quincy, and this is not what it looks like," I said, pointing to the screen. The mint green lacquer on her nails gleamed in my eyes making it difficult for me to formulate a good lie.

"I hope not." Onyjie wagged her head and folded her arms across her chest. "It looks to me like you're cyber stalking him."

My head shook from side to side. There was no real way for me to make an innocent afternoon of research appear innocent. "No, I bumped into him this morning. He gave me his card." This would be a great moment for a genie to pop out and shazaam the card would appear in my hand while Onyjie tapped the toe of her metallic silver booties on the floor waiting to find the hole in my story. I don't know why she went into accounting after college. She has the entire detective thing down pact right down to the cold stare and twisted mouth.

"He's in the industry now."

"What industry? The how-to-get-a-divorce-in-ninety-days industry?" she asked, pointing at Quincy's almond colored face.

"No, the music industry," I said, laughing to disguise my guilt. I had not so much as called him and Onyjie already had me feeling like I was committing adultery.

"Girl, please. He's been in the music industry since you met him like fifteen years ago. It turned out that all he did was hand out flyers for Diddy." Onyjie adjusted her black and white graphic print A-line skirt and parked a quarter of her thigh on my desk.

"Make yourself at home," I offered, sliding the laptop out of the way. "All that street team stuff is in the past. Now he's the boss. He runs MacMusic."

Onyjie shrugged her shoulders and shook her pepper colored pin curls. "Never heard of it. If, and I stress the word, *if*, this is a legitimate recording company, what do you think is going to happen? You cut a demo and then you're going to blow up?"

I lowered my head and focused my eyes on a nick in my new desk to hide my smile. *Was I being naïve in thinking that a chance encounter with my former lover was the key to living my dreams? Well, he wasn't quite a lover. Quincy was more like the love you-leave you-then-love you again type.*

Onyjie seemingly caught onto my quiet contemplation, or my poor avoidance tactics, and snapped my laptop shut. "You better let the past remain in the past."

"I have. It's been ten years since we've even seen each other. I entertained him off and on after we graduated, but once Mason and I got married I cut that off. You're acting like I went and hired a private eye," I said, swatting her hand off my laptop and popping it back open. "I bumped into him at Joe's House of Java."

"Yeah, and Eve bumped into Satan in the garden while she was picking up lunch." Onyjie folded her arms and the corners of her mouth into a scowl at the same time. "You think you're the first pretty girl he's given his card. He probably has two baby mamas and a girlfriend. Don't be no fool, girl."

"Doesn't the bible say you're not supposed to call anyone a fool?" I asked, wagging my pen at her. "There has to be a reason for the past showing up in my present—looking all good. None of this is airbrushed," I explained, pointing at a photo of Quincy. He was seated on the floor of a studio with the tips of his fingers resting on the strings of a guitar positioned on a forty-five degree angle revealing the cuts in his abdomen. I refused to admit that I wasn't sure about Quincy relationship status. That wasn't even something I bothered to consider.

Onyjie took a peek at the screen and poked out her lips, a definite marker of her displeasure. She only poked her lips out like that when one of her dates says they're going dutch or the Chinese restaurant messes up her order. "The last time I checked Mason Seagram, your husband, wasn't lacking anything in the looks department. Don't be no fool and pluck down the roof of your house with your own nails."

I didn't respond right away to make Onyjie think that I took all that "see no evil" preaching she was doing seriously. Looking at a man most certainly was not going to kill me, otherwise I would have been dead on my wedding night. I had no idea that all of Mason's friends were as fine as he is. There is nothing like a brother with a fresh shape up in a well-tailored suit. My wedding party and reception were full of them between Mason's friends from work and his college buddies.

Expelling a shot of air from my nostrils, I looked up at Onyjie, "Dr. Juanita Bynum, are you done preaching? I have work to do," I said, slamming my laptop shut and withdrawing a manila folder from the draw on the right side of my sand colored desk. I swiveled in my chair to place the folder on the credenza. With my back to her I prayed that with all the Holy Ghost wisdom that Onyjie boasted she was full of, she'd take the hint and exit the room. A single woman is the last person I needed telling me how to keep my home in order. It's enough that I have to answer to my mother-in-law, who did not take or did not pass geography because she does not understand what boundaries are. At all.

"All right, sis. I'll get out of your way. But first you have to tell me what kind of hair that is. I like how it's bouncing off your shoulders." She reached over and flicked the toasted bronze ends of my hair with the same pen I'd used to chastise her earlier.

"Mine." I smiled, turning around to face her. Now this was the kind of conversation I could handle.

"If that story gets you through the day, I'm not going to say anything more except you better repent the next time you get on your knees," she said, snapping her fingers. "We still on for lunch?"

"Yes, Onyjie, now scram before someone in accounting reports you to Human Resources for stealing time and I have to draw up a file on you."

"Who's on the chopping block today?" Onyjie tapped her nails on the top of my desk as if that was supposed to be enough to get me to gossip.

"Girl, you know I don't get down like that at work. I'm the director of Human Resources not a journalist on bossip.com. If you want the scoop you're going to have to find out some other way. Now get out of here," I said, shooing Onyjie out of my office.

The click made when the latch met the door strike meant I was finally able to absorb what had transpired today. During a simple daily task performed every day—taking Nathan to school—I'd discovered that the former love of my life was now a successful record company executive and he was still interested in working with me. Lifting the top of my laptop, I rubbed the mouse awakening the screen from sleep mode. I studied the hardened physique that I once cradled on the twin bed of my dorm room, then my gaze shifted to the portrait of Mason and I on our wedding day. Much had changed since then.

By the time Onyjie was knocking on my door with her coat in her hand, I was no closer to understanding why the number one sales leader in the district file was sent to my office. "Girl, are you ready for lunch, or not?" she shouted through the door. "My stomach is growling louder than Lil Jon screaming on a track."

Instead of focusing on the files in front of me I was lost in the thoughts of what would have been, what could have been, and what should be. But that was not about to be the topic of discussion.

"Keep it together, Onyjie, we're still at work," I said while retrieving my faux red leather alligator trench coat. Despite being a certified accountant with an MBA, Onyjie never left the hood at home. It was a gift and a curse. No one in the office messed with her, but everyone talked about her and my affiliation with her. Little did they know, the girl was so saved she wouldn't kill a roach. She was my lifeline back in college when Quincy was busy doing the hokey pokey with my heart.

When I opened the door of my office, Onyjie was leaning

against the wall tapping the pointed toe of her peep toe black ankle booties against the tile.

"Where to?" I asked.

"I'm in the mood for Thai. There's a great place on Forty-fifth and Madison."

My mouth curled in disgust. I had no problem with the Thai food, but the shoulder to shoulder foot traffic of midtown Manhattan at any hour of the day was enough to make me lose my appetite.

"You got something else in mind?" She hooked her arm around mine and dragged me to the elevator bank. "Oh my gosh. I love this." She stroked the sleeve of my trench coat like she was petting a poodle. "Crocodile?"

"Alligator," I whispered in her ear. "It's a knockoff. It's supposed to look like Burberry, but I don't have $115,000 for that."

"Shooot." Onyjie sucked her teeth. "I would have unloaded a stock, a few bonds, and dipped into my IRA for that bad boy." She laughed. "The same way you're careful about your money, is the same way you better be careful with that man," she added with her eyebrow raised and her head on an angle as the silver doors of the elevator parted. "Quincy ain't nothing to play with. I don't want to see you get hurt again."

I stepped back a few inches and stared at her. "Shhh," I said, pressing my finger to my lips. Everyone at Cloud Nine did not need to know I was having drama in my marriage especially when I wasn't. Okay, maybe I was a little bit; however, that's not public information.

"Girl, please; they don't know you. Excuse me," Onyjie said, tapping a man on the shoulder who had his face focused on the screen of his tablet. "Do you know who she is?" she asked, pointing at me. The man scrunched up his face and hunched his shoulders. "Is there anyone on this elevator who knows this woman's name," Onyjie asked loud enough for the other seven people on the elevator to hear.

Not one person knew my name.

"No one knows the people in HR until they have to go to HR.

Trust me, the only people concerned about your business right now is Jesus and me."

Chapter 4

For the entire duration of our lunch, Onyjie voiced all of her and Jesus' concerns about my marriage. Never in my life had I been so ecstatic to return to work and review an employee's file. The elevator doors rolled back revealing glints of gold and the shine of freshly washed glass, signaling we'd arrived at the tenth floor. I exhaled a sharp breath, issued Onyjie a dry goodbye, and wriggled through the small pockets of space without waiting for anyone to move. Rubbing against the bodies of my co-workers made my stomach churn, but not as much as Onyjie's marital advice did. Her constant harping on the pitfalls of engaging in an adulterous relationship left a nasty taste in my mouth. Not even an entire glass of the sweetest Thai iced tea in New York City could make it go away.

By the end of lunch I was annoyed with her presumptuous attitude and defense of Mason. The more I thought about it the quicker my steps became. The click clack of my heels down the glittering hall that led to the HR department became the rhythm that accompanied the riff of thoughts in my head. She did not understand what it was like being married to a man who was dead set on becoming the next Hezekiah Walker. It all sounded like a dream to her—the glazed over look in her eyes each time she talked about my relationship with Mason was a dead giveaway. However admirable Mason's aspirations for his music ministry were, they were not my goals, and I didn't know why I had to absorb them and become his sidekick. When we married he'd promised we'd be like Ashford and Simpson—madly in love and married to the music.

When I rounded the corner Meena, my secretary, was standing in front of her desk smiling and waving at me. Her attentiveness and bright smile cut right into my investigation into why my marriage was beginning to fail.

"Hi, Meena. Did you miss me?" I asked, referring to the way she was waiting to greet me like a lap dog.

"Mrs. Seagram, you're so funny," she said, swiping her wispy brunette hair out of her eyes. "I'm so excited to see you because I can't wait to see the look on your face when you go into your office."

"Ugh." I groaned, letting my arms droop at my sides. "You didn't redecorate again, did you?"

"No. While you were at lunch you received a delivery and it's mighty extravagant. I hope that after I've been married for ten years my husband still does things like Mr. Seagram."

"Thank you, Meena. I'm sure it's nothing out of the ordinary," I said as I walked past her desk. I turned the knob and my stomach dropped to my heels. On the other side of the door a tall medley of flowers and fruit curled into a G clef awaited me. A smile spread across my face as I approached this massive fruit salad structure. I fingered the petals of the black orchids and inspected the assortment of fruits—pineapple chunks, mangoes, and strawberries covered in white chocolate. All of my favorite things were neatly assembled on my desk. Mason must have thought there was another dog sniffing around his backyard.

"Excuse me," I said to Meena who was still standing in the doorway gawking at the flowers as I picked up the phone and dialed Mason's cell phone number.

He probably thought this massive floral arrangement would get me to join the choir and keep my affections at home. I would have preferred some new shoes. Shoot, for a new pair of Fendi pumps I'd churn out "I Go to the Rock" in a heartbeat and have them saints running up and down the aisle of our church in a minute.

"Praise the Lord!" Mason shouted into the phone when he answered. *Why did he have to be all holy all the time?*

"Hello, Mason."

"What's going on, my love? You usually don't call me in the middle of the day."

"You tell me what's going on, Mason. Do you think that a little gallant gesture and some white chocolate will get me to work on the record with your choir?"

"What are you talking about?"

"You know exactly what I'm talking about. The floral arrangement—"

"Floral arrangement?" he queried, cutting me off.

"If you thought that an oversized wreath would get me to sing with that little gospel choir of yours, you're wrong."

"Kira, I did not send you any floral arrangement."

Half listening to his spiel, I dug my hand into the center of the arrangement and removed the card. *Without your voice my music is all blues and no rhythm. ~Q*

I read the message again and flashes of heat coursed through my fingers. His vulnerability was sexy. Quincy McAdams had gone from a chemistry major to a music mogul and his life was still missing something. The words on the card spoke louder to me than Mason until he shouted into the receiver,

"Well, where did the flowers come from? I will not ask again."

"Calm down, Daddy," I said, trying to lay on the sex appeal real thick. I needed a dollop strong enough to coat the lie I was about to tell, "It was a mistake. These flowers were delivered to the wrong office."

"I'm glad we solved the mystery of the flowers," Mason laughed softly before saying he had to go.

Instead of investigating why Jeffrey Henson, the strongest marketing associate we had, file was on my desk I devoted most of my afternoon to walking back and forth through my office contemplating whether I should call Quincy and thank him for the wreath.

Once I determined that a phone call couldn't be that dangerous,

I slicked back the mound of curls that encased my face, picked up the receiver, and called the number he'd given me after our reunion near our kids' school. I drummed on the keyboard in front of me while I waited for him to answer the phone. After a few rings I planned what I would say on his voicemail. I didn't want to sound too eager or impressed by the flowers or desperate for stardom.

"What's up KK?" he cooed into the phone startling me. I paused for a moment before responding. A short wave of heat encompassed me, cutting off my breath. No one called me that except Quincy, and I had not realized until this moment how much those two letters meant.

"KK, are you there?"

"How did you know it was me?"

"The caller ID says Cloud Nine Studios. You're the only person I know at Cloud Nine with my personal cell phone number."

"Your personal number. You gave me your personal number?"

"Yes, I want to do more than just business with you."

"Really?" I asked, trying not to engage in the flirtatious banter he'd initiated.

"Really. It's been a long time since we got together. I was hoping to catch up, like over dinner this evening. You still have a sweet tooth?"

I pursed my lips together to keep the tender giggle he inspired in my throat when I thought about how Quincy discovered my sweet tooth. The Lord blessed me with a neat hourglass shape that concealed my love of all things filled with sugar. I'd never meant for Quincy to find out about it either, but after several all-night tutoring sessions for my chemistry class I had to reveal my secrets. By the fourth night I popped open the lock box I kept under my bed and tossed a package of gummi worms and peanut M&Ms at him.

"You can do the honors tonight," I'd said.

"What is this?" he'd asked, staring at his hands.

"What does it look like, fool?"

"Well, most people keep guns in lock boxes, not candy." He'd ripped the gummi bears open with his gleaming white teeth.

"Let's just say I gave you a little something from my personal stash."

Quincy raised his dark chocolate eyes and met mine. The intensity of his eyes was like a magician's cape, they made the entire room disappear. The dull beige of the walls and the stiff, flat pale orange carpet vanished. The chorus of Amerie's "One Thing" seeped through the thin dormitory walls silencing the gurgle of my mini-fridge. Quincy approached me from behind.

"Thank you," he'd said, resting his hand on the small of my waist. His touch seemed innocent, so I let his hand remain.

"For?" I'd asked, looking back at him over my shoulder. *"I ought to thank you for helping me tonight."* I secured my lockbox of candy. When I turned around he was standing right in front of me. He traced the apple of my right cheek and the side of my face until he reached my chin. I shuddered as his fingertips grazed my skin. Quincy's touch was soft and hypnotic just like the scent of his ocean breeze cologne that danced through the stale air of my room.

"I'm sorry," he'd said, looking away as soon as my eyes caught his. *"I shouldn't…"*

I don't know whether it was the Boy Scout look on his face, the way his brown skin glowed in the hunter crew neck shirt, or I was still reeling from his touch. My lips silenced his apology. First a light grazing, then another. Quincy grabbed my shoulders, "What are you doing, KK?"

"I don't know," I'd responded, pecking him on the lips again. *"But your lips taste so sweet and I have a sweet tooth."* There was something comforting and familiar about Quincy that just drew me into him.

As the memory of our first kiss manifested before my eyes I knew that admitting I still have a sweet tooth could prove to be dangerous especially since it's been a long while since Mason has done a single thing to satisfy it.

"I may," I said, snapping out of my jog up memory lane.

"Well, let's do dinner at the Sugar Factory tonight and talk about you, me, and your demo."

"Demo?"

"You still got those pipes made of gold?"

"You know I do," I replied, breaking out into a smile.

"Give me a little something before I go."

I put the phone down and placed Quincy on speaker before rattling off a little riff. "I want to be in a place. In a place where I can see your smiling face and all of my pain will dissipate."

Quincy hummed and added a little run to what I was doing and then shouted, "Enough. I get it. You still got it and I can't wait to do something with it."

Chapter 5

During the train ride downtown to Manhattan's Meat Packing District I imagined quashing every romantic advance that Quincy made across the dinner table. But, I didn't have to worry about the possibility of romance being a part of this dinner. The Sugar Factory was so sweet that every square foot of the place was occupied. The bar stools were covered with alpha males and their arm candy or at least potential arm candy. Since it was early evening the candy shop contained a mixture of tourist and cute couples taking selfies and stuffing bags with old-fashioned candy. The hostess requested that only those with a reservation step up to the podium.

"If your date doesn't show, you can sit at my table," Quincy breathed into my ear. The tip of his lip grazed my ear.

"Did you get a reservation or not?" I said over my shoulder trying to avoid eye contact or the slightest elevations in my pitch to slip and let him know that the candy in this place wasn't the only sweet thing.

"You know I'm always prepared," he said, squeezing my waistline.

I turned and faced him. He had to be crazy hugging me in public like we were still together. "What the heck are you doing?" I pried his hands off my waist. "I'm not one of those record industry groupies. I don't know why you think you can just grope me."

He smiled and wiped the tip of his concave nose. "I thought we had a bond." His smile widened. "And you look ravishing in red." He pulled me into his body, using the belt of my coat like a fishing reel.

"I'm married. You are aware of that, aren't you?"

"That's just a technicality. Shhh…" He placed a finger over my lips before I could even think of a response. Quincy flagged the hostess with one arm and placed his other free arm in a more appropriate location—around my shoulder. "Quincy McAdams," he shouted at the hostess above the raised voices and giggles.

The hostess beckoned us to come forward and led us to a booth with thick, dark leather seats.

"Your server will be with you shortly. Would you like some drinks to get you started?"

"Do you still like gummy bears?" he asked.

I bobbed my head up and down. "Please bring us an Energy Bear and two straws."

Instantly a server returned with a sixty-ounce goblet of pink vapor with Gummy bears and two straws floating in the glass, placing it between us.

"Q, what is this?"

"The Energy Bear, a sweet libation full of gummy bears and a shot of Red Bull. Forget about your husband. Don't bother to check your phone. Tonight it's just you and me."

"I thought this was supposed to be about the music. Your baby mama and the stable of women you keep wouldn't want you smiling in my face and filling my belly with drinks." I poked my straw into the glass and took a sip. The stinging bite of vodka rested in my throat followed by a sweet aftertaste of what had to be created by Haribo Gummy Bears floating around in the glass.

"This is about the music. You're the one making it about more, and I only have one child with one woman since you're fishing." He laughed and caught my eye with his gaze. "I always have dinner with an artist before I take them on."

"Take…me…on…" I choked on the liquor gathered in my mouth. I'd heard God worked in mysterious ways, but this seemed a little too sudden for it to just be the work of the Lord.

"Yeah… take you on…" He folded his hands in front of

him. "It occurred to me after we got off the phone that it made absolutely no sense for me to be helping you cut a demo for you to shop around with my competitors when I was the first one to discover those pipes." Quincy stopped his manifest destiny speech and planted his straw into our shared libation. He stirred the ice with his straw before vacuuming up a third of the drink. "It would be stupid of me to lose you twice."

"Twice?"

"Yeah…I already let another man marry you. There's no way I'm going to let another record company have you. MacMusic is your new home."

Either it was his words or the three colossal-sized drinks I'd had over dinner. I smiled as the warmth his words created in me spread through each ligament of my body as we headed to his car.

"Don't look at me like that," Quincy said, turning his face away from my gaze.

The culprit was still a mystery; however, passion was breaking out all over my body. I couldn't help but sit in the seat with an extra curve in the arch of my back and every sentence ended with me biting down on my bottom lip. I ignored his request. I continued to concentrate my gaze on his profile.

A slight wash of burgundy covered his cheeks.

"I'm tempted to touch you, right now." I leaned back in my seat and closed my eyes. I couldn't believe those coconut oil slick words had come out of my mouth. It had been a long time since we were in close proximity to each other. I realized that dinner probably wasn't a good idea nor was having Quincy drive me home. I could hear Onyjie in my head reprimanding me. After only one meal I was one foot away from ending up like Bathsheba.

When I opened my eyes his austere russet brown eyes confronted me. His eyes were more forceful than his words. They held me captive and sped up the cadence of my heartbeat.

"I hate to admit it, KK, but I'm feeling just as tempted," he said, gripping the leather steering wheel tightly.

My eyes traveled up his lengthy arm and studied his face. I absorbed every line on his face including the small nick on his chin.

"What happened?" I asked, tracing the nick with the tip of my finger.

Quincy grabbed my hand and pressed it to his face. He closed his eyes and reclined in the ivory leather seats of his Range Rover. Before I could stop him, he brought my hand to his curved sugary lips and kissed my wrist.

"What are you doing?" I asked, snatching my hand back.

Quincy grabbed for my hand again and this time he placed it against his heart which was beating rapidly to a rhythm that only he heard.

"Kira," he began, his voice laced with sugar.

I looked away before answering, "Quincy." I attempted to keep my eyes on the cherry blossom blooms as they fell and gathered into a pile in the gutter a few feet away from the passenger side window. Just above the tree I watched as the wind forced a lily in my window box of flowers to bend.

I realized then I was parked a few steps from my home—from my front door—with Quincy kissing my wrist. Every drop of romance and mystique was sucked out of the air by that realization and the stale scent of guilt filled the air and fogged up his tinted windows.

"Quincy, what do you think you're doing?" I snatched my hand back again. "My husband is just a few feet away."

"I'm sorry, Kira," he said, blushing. He lowered his lids like he'd been caught pilfering change from his mother's purse. "I was trying to behave, but you emit something—"

"No, no, no," I interjected with my palm raised in his face. "Don't you get into all of that 'my neutrons are attracting your protons' stuff you used to use on me when we were in college." I tried to use some couth to remind him that what we had was in the past and remind myself of my present. I'm a grown woman with a husband and son to think about. Late night rendezvous in Range Rovers were no longer an option for me.

"What kind of man..." he lowered his hand and reached across the width of the car to rub the base of my chin with the knuckles of his pointer and middle fingers. "What kind of man would I be if I didn't try? I thought I saw a little flint in your eyes inviting me in."

"Well, forget about what you thought you saw and you can forget about me coming to the studio with you," I blurted while attempting to push the door open. It was supposed to be a grand and dramatic exit except the door wouldn't open. "Can you open the door?"

"Sorry. Child safety locks. Gwen likes to sit in the front with me," he explained while pushing some buttons on the console of his dashboard. "You're free to go now, but," he caught the sleeve of my coat in his hand, "please say you'll come to the studio with me. Ever since I had it built I have imagined what you would sound like in the booth riding one of my tracks."

I opened my mouth to shut him down, and he responded, "I promise I'll be a good boy."

"Best behavior?"

"No doubt," he said and bowed his head before releasing me. "Best behavior."

Chapter 6

"Where have you been?" Mason's question greeted me at the door.

I hadn't thought about how I was going explain this evening away. The liquor was easy. I could chalk that up to an after work event. There was always something to celebrate at Cloud Nine—between Golden Globe nominations or the premiere of a new show. Something was always going on. Even though Mason didn't agree with me drinking, and most often he met me with a proverb, *wine is a mocker and strong drink is a raging, whosoever is deceived by them is not wise*, I could still argue that it was for work and not for pleasure. I tiptoed around Mason and Nate's shoes and hoped that tonight my "when in Rome" story would suffice.

"Where's Nate?" I asked once I reached the living room. I knew the answer already. Nate went to bed at eight every night. That was a well-known fact throughout Harlem, I'm sure. Nine year olds today didn't just drift off to sleep with little coaxing, but Nate differed from most nine year olds. Mason sat in his favorite thinking chair—a charcoal laz-e-boy we'd scored for half price at a Black Friday sale a few years ago. A look of solemnity controlled the muscles of his face and arranged them into a grimace. If thinking was what he wanted to do, I knew I needed to move his thoughts into another direction and off the fact that I was creeping in after ten o'clock.

"In bed." He folded his hands across his chest and interlocked his fingers. "He's not feeling well. I think he's about to experience another crisis."

Mason always referred to Nate's illness as a doctor would—technical and distant—because he'd never had to clean the vomit or rush him to the hospital at the onset of a fever. Ever since Nate was diagnosed with Sickle Celle Anemia, it felt like my life was in a perpetual state of crisis. Unlike Mason, I don't get to retreat into my prayer closet and claim I was there for Nate. Motherhood required I be present for every moment.

"I think he should stay home tomorrow," Mason suggested, interrupting my silent complaint.

Mason relaxed further into his chair. His thick, long locs adorned his shoulders. His scruffy beard made him look a few years older than thirty-eight. The possibility that this was tougher for Mason than he wanted me to believe occurred to me as I took in his posture and the sullen expression he wore. Lost in thought. His sleek, ebony cheekbones raised and his eyes fell into sharp slits.

"I'm nervous…" He paused and the corners of his mouth turned down. "Maybe my little prophet ought to stay home. Well, what do you think, Mrs. Seagram?" Mason sat upright in his chair and waved his hand at me.

"You're overreacting," I said, responding to his initial concern.

"I could be overreacting or our son is getting sick."

"If you're that concerned, why don't you stay home with him?" I tried to throw that question out without it sounding like an accusation, but I guess seeing me with my hands on my hip must still put Mason on the defensive.

He hoped out of his seat and planted himself in front of me. He slid his arms through the diamond arcs my arms created, cupped my waist, and pulled me into him. "You know that if I could spend a thousand days without going anywhere, I would." He caressed my cheek. "If I could utter one word that would heal our son, I would. And if I believed for one second that me staying home instead of fulfilling my service to the Lord could help then I would stay here."

"What about what I want?"

Mason's eyebrows drew together and he spit his words out like the thought of what he was saying tasted bad. "You want to go to work more than you want to stay home with our son. That job has got your brain completely warped."

"Don't make this about my job, Mase."

"What do you want it to be about? Your wants and desires?" he asked.

My head throbbed. Cloud Nine had become Mason's scapegoat for everything that was wrong in our home. He always seemed to forget or found a way to overlook the fact that I was so invested in Cloud Nine because he'd taken his foot and stomped all over my dreams and replaced them with his. Through my nostrils I sucked in enough air to fill a hot air balloon and shut my mouth. There was no way I would let him ruin this moment. I'd just sealed the deal with Quincy that I'd been waiting my whole life for. The record deal that Mason had promised we'd have when we met at the Apollo. It was a corny thing to do, but I figured signing up for Amateur Night at the Apollo couldn't hurt my career. At the end of my number he was waiting for me in the wings with a slight grin on his face. "I think I'm in love," he'd breathed, reaching for my arm.

"You barely know me."

"But I know what I heard and I want to know more." He'd cupped my elbow and pulled me in close. I didn't know if it was his aggression or the glints of passion I saw in his eyes, but I was gone. All I wanted to do was sing but Mason wouldn't let me. We waned and loafed around his studio apartment writing love songs and eating ramen noodles until reality set in. Now here we were, far from the passion and far from the lights. He had not made good on his promises of stardom yet and once again he was asking me to sacrifice for our family.

"Our walk with Christ isn't about what we want," Mason replied before leaning in to kiss me. His pious lips seemed to sizzle upon contact. *Maybe that was guilt burning me up.*

Mason stepped back and focused his eyes on mine, which were zigzagging all over the living room. I hadn't fixed my eyes on a thing since I walked in to avoid that spirit of discernment every minister seems to have. The intensity of his deep set doe eyes drew me in. My head bobbed back and I allowed my eyes to meet his gaze. Mason tapped my lips twice with his lips and continued. "Serving Christ is about doing His will, not our own. Whatever you decide is fine, but I trust that you'll make the decision that puts our son's health ahead of your career." Mason kissed me one more time.

The weight of his kiss and the warmth of his touch forced me to try and figure out a way to cancel on Quincy without having to forfeit my final chance at recording—at least with a major label. Mason and his gospel troupe would always have a spot for me, but I wasn't trying to perform at McDonald's Mother's Day gospel concert. This voice was built for Madison Square Garden and perfected for sold out shows at the Barclay, the newest arena in New York. As good as my voice was, I was not a fool. There's an expiration date on everything and mine was fast approaching. I took in my reflection in the mirror that lined the hallway. At thirty-seven I could still pass for a twenty-something, especially as hard as some of these girls looked nowadays, but no one is checking for a thirty-something pop star who needed her roots died and ends trimmed. Quincy was my way in—the open door that Pastor Stone had preached about on Sunday.

I tried to recall the rest of her sermon while I walked to Nate's bedroom to check on my young prince. As usual, he'd fallen asleep with the light on and a bunch of Pokémon cards by his side. I picked the cards up in the exact order I found them in, to keep from getting in trouble. The last time I stacked up Nate's cards incorrectly, I upset the balance of some furball's powers and he lost the game. His oval shaped face had the resplendent glow of a little chocolate angel. Nights like this his illness didn't sit right in my gut.

I watched his chest rise and fall and listened to the hum of his breath. When he was sick his breathing always gave it away between the rattling sound and scent. I no longer needed a doctor to diagnose what was wrong with my son. What Nate needed wasn't another day off from school. He needed a healing. The one I'd been waiting on since he was diagnosed.

The heat and the hurt of the moment collapsed on my chest and pulled me to my knees. I withdrew my cell phone and sent a text message to Quincy. The thought of my son hurting was harder to take than a flurry of Mayweather punches.

"Father, I don't know what you're waiting for, but I'd like

deliverance for my son." I stroked the crown of his head and used his bed as a springboard to lift myself up.

I repositioned myself on the edge of his bed and watched him for a few minutes. "I'm sorry that I gave you this disease," I said aloud, recalling my first contact I had with sickle cell anemia. I shook my head to ward off the memory of the days I suffered with migraines and nausea because I had the trait. People tried to calm my mother by reminding her it was only "the trait" and not the full blown disease. It should have been comforting, but I was accident-prone and a hypochondriac. We lived in the hospital and when we were at home she shuffled back and forth between my bedroom and the laundry room. Kangaroo pouches sat under her eyes and a deep-seeded hatred for my father, who could come and go as he pleased, lived in her eyes.

"Oh, Lord please take this curse from him."

"It's not a curse, Ma," Nate mumbled, his eyes still closed.

"Nate, were you awake this whole time?" I asked, squeezing the tip of his arrowhead nose.

"I didn't hear you come in but…I heard you praying." He propped himself up and rested on his elbow. "It's not your fault, Mom. I talked with my biology teacher and he said that you and Daddy both had to have the defective gene for me to inherit this disease. You are both to blame for this."

"Oh, yeah?" I smiled at how knowledgeable he was about his own disease.

"Yeah, Mom. You know what else I learned today?"

"What?"

"Daddy chose my name because Nathan was the name of the prophet the Lord sent to correct David in his sin. That's why I corrected you just now. I'm practicing. Daddy said you have to do what you want to do tomorrow, today."

"So, do you want to be a prophet or you want to go around correcting people?"

Nathan chuckled a little. "Mom, you know what I mean."

"I think I do, small-fry," I said, smoothing down the crown of his hair. "I didn't come in here to disturb you. Your dad said you're not feeling well. He thinks you should stay home from school tomorrow."

"Ma, I can't keep running from this thing. On Sunday I heard the pastor talking about the thorn in Paul's flesh. Paul still did his work with that thorn in his flesh. I think I'm supposed to keep on going too, even though this bothers me."

"Nuff said, prophet." I cupped his face and kissed him on the forehead. Relief caressed my heart. Nathan was growing in the word of God and trying to live by it. For the moment he felt invincible and capable of carrying on. With that realization I knew that I needed to carry on. If I didn't have to stay home with Nate I would follow my dream wherever it led me.

"Are you sure you don't want to stay home?" I asked as I stood to leave.

"Definitely," he said, nodding and grinning.

I blew him one more kiss before exiting his room. Outside of his bedroom door I whipped out my cellphone and texted Quincy again.

It's on. See you at the studio.

Chapter 7

After I dropped Nate off at his school, I drove to Quincy's Chelsea studio. The hunt for parking amid the trucks and early morning traffic on a Tuesday was fruitless. I should have taken the subway like a normal New Yorker, but then I wouldn't have had the opportunity to get into my zone. I blasted Beyoncé during the drive to Chelsea. It was a guilty pleasure I hid from Mason. There was no use for a singer with a love for the secular world in his choir, but today I'd have something to show him.

Quincy was in the middle of mixing a track when I entered the studio. He strummed the wood grain on the boards with his left hand and his foot tapped out the slow and heavy beat. The vocals were hard to hear. It sounded like a breathy young Toni Braxton imitator moaning over the track. He didn't look up or acknowledge me in any way. Instead he scooted in closer to the boards, hovered over it, and manipulated the beat until the vibrancy of desire flooded out of the speakers.

I didn't know what to make of the atmosphere. The smell of cottonwood accompanied by dim lights and Quincy's straight back and broad shoulders were a combination for baby making not music making. "Oh… please, God keep me," I whispered into the air under my breath. I had to call in for backup because I wasn't sure I would be able to keep it together. My insides felt like candle wax melting, and had Quincy's assistant not turned around and said something I would have been all over his neck like aftershave.

"He doesn't like people standing over him while he's mixing," the sound engineer declared before turning back around to face the boards.

"KK," Quincy said without looking up, "I'll be with you in a minute. This track is almost done."

I took a few steps back and sat on the couch behind us.

"Raoul." Quincy tapped the engineer on the shoulder. "Drop the base and let her ad libs ride the song out."

"You wild, boy." Raoul punched Quincy in the arm. "This joint right here will be bumping everywhere." Raoul spun around and looked me up and down. "I don't know if you can blow or you're just another pretty face—we get plenty of those trying to creep up in here—but you're lucky. More like you're blessed to work with Q. You're in good hands."

"Say that one more time," Quincy said, his smile wide enough to be spotted from behind.

"You're in good hands," Raoul repeated.

Quincy rotated his chair in my direction. "I've been trying to tell you that I will take care of you, KK," he said, smiling. As if the wattage of his smile and the words of some strange guy were supposed to be enough for me to just relax and begin recording. Just looking into his eyes makes me feel so close to damnation. I've spent plenty of time around handsome men with power. Quincy McAdams and that glowing stare of his shouldn't be enough to move me, but maybe it was Onyjie's preaching on Monday evening that had me messed up. When I told her I was taking a day off from work for this, she started speaking in tongues and rebuking me. I tried to maintain my professionalism to keep our friendship intact, so I didn't let the cursing demon in me out.

"How are you?" Quincy asked, using his eyes to probe me.

"What?" I asked. I wasn't sure if he was trying to assess my mental state to record or just trying to be cordial. All I wanted to do was get my business taken care of and make it out of the building without compromising my marriage and the little bit of faith I had left.

"How are you?" he repeated, scooting over in the chair. After two short scoots he was breathing over me. The tips of his fingers met mine. "How are you feeling?" he asked, making eye contact.

"I'm tired, Quincy. Nate's not feeling well. He may need to be hospitalized, but right now he's claiming that everything is fine and I…" my head dropped along with my voice. A cry was trying to rise within me and I'd promised myself last year I'd given up crying about this situation.

Quincy covered my hands with his and rubbed the side of my face with his like a cat rubbing against his master's leg. I peeked at Raoul who was still working on the track. Raoul seemed unfazed by our exchange taking place behind his back.

"Raoul," Quincy called out, seemingly noticing my discomfort. "Would you give me a moment?"

"Q, I'm almost done."

"Give me a minute, starting now," he commanded. His usually soft voice now boomed throughout the room. Quincy held up one finger. "Give me a minute."

Raoul backed out the room, but not without reminding us both of the reason we were there. "Boss, time is money."

"And money is time," Quincy replied. "I got plenty of money, so that means I got plenty of time."

"True dat," Raoul said and exited.

A hush fell over the studio. Nothing could be heard except our breaths. Mine was heavy and slow and a rhythmic low hum escaped from Quincy.

"Kids get sick all the time." He drew my hands to his mouth and kissed them.

"He's not sick…" I pulled my hands back. I hate it when people equated Nate's illness with the common cold. A ten dollar bottle of Nyquil didn't take the pain away. "He has Sickle Cell Anemia."

Quincy bit down on his bottom lip and cleared his throat. His eyes shifted from my face to his hands and back again. "Is it the trait, or the full blown disease?"

Now it was my turn to look away. There'd been no retreat or resting place for me since Nate's diagnosis. "My son may not live past the age of forty." A thin film of water lined my eyelid. *I will not cry here. In front of this man.*

I'd almost gotten the not crying thing down pact. The expectation was black women were strong and my God even stronger, so if I just turned it all over to Him there'd be nothing to worry about. Even my mother had tried to inject that *Jesus wouldn't give me more than I could bare.* I searched the Bible for that scripture; it turns out I Corinthians 10:13 said, *There has no temptation taken you but such as is common to man: but God is faithful, who will not allow you to be tempted above that you are able; but will with the temptation also make a way to escape, that you may be able to bear it.* Which didn't explain how to bear nursing a sick child, nor did it give me the strength I needed to look into his yellowing eyes and feed him the same lie I had to suck on—everything will be all right. At this moment though, I needed to be kept because Quincy's unblinking eye, seeming concern, and strong jaw was very tempting.

"There's nothing for you to worry about." He traced my jawline from cheek to chin with one finger and tipped my head up. "Nate seems like he's a strong kid."

I jerked my head back. *How much interaction did he have with my son?*

"Stop squinting at me like that," Quincy commanded. "Just grilling me isn't going to get you the answer to your question."

"What question?" I asked, rolling my eyes. It should have been impossible for him to still read me like that after ten years. It would be nice if my supposed king could read me like that. However, his discerning spirit only worked when I was hiding shoes that weren't in my budget for the month. We weren't doing badly, but we weren't doing well, either.

"Come on," he chided. "I know something is percolating in that nugget." Quincy tapped my temple like he was checking whether or not I was a ripe coconut.

"How long have you known that my son attended Emblem Academy?"

Quincy cocked his head to the side and grinned at me. His smile was daubed in guilt.

I could almost hear the story he was fabricating in his head before he spoke. He shifted the position of his legs. I guess he had to get comfortable to tell this tale. He propped one leg on the black matte plastic that covered the wheels of the chair, then stretched his other leg straight out and adjusted the monumental diamond encrusted letter Q that hung from the platinum chain around his neck.

"Quincy Ezekiel McAdams."

Hearing his full name jolted Quincy out of his thoughts and he popped up like frozen waffles in the toaster.

"Stop fidgeting and fishing for a story in that big head of yours," I demanded, plucking him on the forehead. I don't know how I remembered that he fidgeted when he was about to tell a lie and most certainly didn't know why I could recall his entire name after all this time.

"It's irrelevant." He rolled up in front of me, cocked his legs open, and sandwiched my legs between his.

I blinked my eyes as rapidly as I could to avoid getting caught up in the trance he was trying to put me under. The music—I'm here for the music.

He rested his hands on my thighs. "All that matters," he dropped his head down to meet my eyes, "is we found each other," he said before leaning in and kissing me.

I wanted to pull back but the magnetism of his kiss kept me frozen in time. He stroked the back of my neck with one hand and squeezed my thigh with the other. My flesh quivered in his hand like jelly. My body buckled and surrendered to him even though my spirit kept nudging me to stand up.

Thankfully, my cell phone rang. With a slight shift in my posture, I pulled my head back and took the call.

"Yes, this is Mrs. Seagram." I shot him the one raised eyebrow stare. "The hospital…Okay … There's no need to call my husband I will… I'm on my way." After disconnecting with Nate's school nurse, I jammed my cell phone back into my bag.

"What happened, KK? Talk to me." He rubbed his goatee and stared at me like I owed him something.

"No. You tell me something. What the heck was that?" I asked, slapping his chest out of frustration. "What was that, Quincy?" I hopped to my feet and slung my purse over my shoulder. "Oh, just forget it. I don't have time for sympathy or romantic musings. That was the school. Nate passed out and they're taking him to the hospital."

"Which one? I'll take you."

"I came in my car; there's no need for that. I don't need the kind of help you're offering," I declared, backing away.

"I'm sorry." Quincy grabbed my wrist. "But there's something here... you make my belly burn." He lowered his eyes and rubbed the back of his neck, "What do you want me to do?"

I snatched my arm from his grip. "If your belly is burning that's called indigestion. I'm sorry, but you're going to have to accept things the way they are," I said before running out the studio.

Chapter 8

Tuesday must be a high emergency day. The ER at St. Luke's hospital was standing room only. My attempt to get to the triage window was thwarted by a bike messenger near the rear of the line. "Hey, lady, there's a line and you better get in it," he shouted at me waving his bloodied and scar-covered arm.

"I'm not trying to cut the line. My son is here."

"Oh, my fault, Ms." He bowed apologetically and screamed at the others in line. "Let her through. Her son is back there. Come on y'all, back it up and let this lady through," he demanded. At his request everyone in line, from the old lady bent over her walker to the man clutching his chest, slid to the right and allowed me access to the triage nurse. For the most part, New Yorkers were as rude and as aggressive as people thought, but for a mother and child, even a monstrous bike messenger turned into a warring angel.

"Ms. just sign your name on the list. There's no reason for you to approach the window unless your name is called," the nurse said without so much as lifting her eyes from her computer screen.

"My son was brought here via ambulance and I need to see him now," I shouted, pounding on the Plexiglas that separated us.

Either my tone of voice or that bang on the glass was enough to remind her of her course in bedside manner. "I'm so sorry about that, ma'am," she cooed.

I cut her off as she attempted to deliver an explanation that sounded like a stream of running water.

"My son's name is Nathan Seagram."

She took her glasses off of her head and punched in his name in the computer. "Are you Kira Seagram?"

I nodded my head.

"We've been expecting you. I will buzz you in. Push the door to the left when you see the green light go off," she instructed me. "Follow the red tape on the floor to the Pediatric ER."

When the green light went off I ran down the corridor, allowing the red tape to direct my path until I ran into a group of doctors.

"Are you all right?" the doctor I collided with asked.

"Yes, I'm trying to get to my son, Nathan Seagram."

"No problem, I'll take you to him," the doctor offered, breaking away from the pack.

"How is he?"

He smiled and adjusted the stethoscope wrapped around his neck. "Ms. Seagram, I'm Doctor Lipal, and I've been attending to your son since his arrival. He's a strong boy." Dr. Lipal placed his hand on my shoulder. "Nate will be okay. It won't be necessary for him to stay overnight; however, he will need bed rest and a trip to his regular doctor as soon as possible, Mom."

"What's wrong with him, doctor?"

"Let's walk and discuss this," he said, guiding me toward the pediatric ER.

"No. You're going to tell me right now what's going on with my son so I can pull it together before I have to face him. He was brought here in an ambulance." My lips trembled. "They said he passed out in school. Everything will not be okay," I said between sniffs.

"Listen, Mom."

"I'm not your mother. My name is Mrs. Seagram," I declared. "I'm Nate's mother, so let's please stop beating around the bush."

Dr. Lipal cleared his throat. "It appears as though your son has leg ulcers. It's still early so his doctor will be able to do something about it."

"Leg ulcers?" I was stunned. I knew that was one complication that sometimes accompanied sickle cell anemia, but I hadn't prepared for my son to have them. "Isn't that usually a complication affecting adults with Sickle Cell?" I asked.

"It impacts adults, but acute leg ulcers can form in patients as early as ten years old."

I closed my eyes and asked God, *Why my son? Why now?*

"It seems as though he is near stage three. There's been some damage to his skin tissue."

My head dropped back, and I covered my mouth with my hand to keep my scream bottled up. Leg ulcers were for adults not cute nine year olds. Not my son. After taking a few deep breaths, I uncovered my mouth and asked, "What caused him to pass out?"

"The pain. Leg ulcers can cause debilitating pain, especially for a child when they haven't been treated."

To harvest the energy necessary to comfort Nate I took a few more deep breaths. "May I see him now?"

"Of course you can. Are you ready?"

"This is what I do." I shook my head and straightened my shoulders, mostly to convince myself that this was something I could handle.

When we arrived at Nate's bed, a nurse was placing fresh bandages on his wounds. So far there were three on his right thigh. Craters marked his left calf. They made his leg look like the surface of the moon. The skin surrounding the craters was cracked and inflamed. I looked up to Dr. Lipal who'd kept his eyes zoomed in on me since we pulled back the curtain.

"Hi, Ma," Nate chirped from his bed with a sweet smile.

I don't know how he could smile while he looked like a zombie from "The Walking Dead" had attacked him. "Nate, how long have your legs been like this?" I asked, pointing to his bandage.

"It's no big deal, Ma." He shrugged his shoulders and looked at the nurse, and then Dr. Lipal. As if they could save him from the boiling water he'd just placed himself in by hiding something like this from me.

"What you looking at her for?" I asked, pointing at the nurse. "Don't even look at him," I stated in a tone that scared even me. *Don't get crazy.* "Doctor, please give us a moment?"

Dr. Lipal bowed in concession and backed out right through a sliver of space where the wall and curtain almost met. The nurse remained, but she didn't say a word giving us a pseudo-sense of privacy.

"What the heck do you mean, no big deal?" I tried to coax myself into taking it easy, but him hiding stuff like this could be life threatening. "Acne is no big deal. Holes in your leg are a big deal."

Nate's nose wrinkled and his thick eyebrows drew close together. The pensive expression that had taken over his face made him look just like Mason right before he was about to go into prayer warrior mode. "Ma, I didn't want you going crazy like you are now."

"Crazy? You haven't seen crazy yet. Wait 'til I get a hold of your father. If he's been helping you hide this… oww… when did this start?"

He glanced at the nurse again. "Don't look at her." I poked my chin out in the nurse's direction, "Answer me. When did this start?"

"Like two months ago. It's no big deal—it's part of my condition."

"How do you know that?"

"I looked it up on Google, Ma." He smiled at the nurse then at me, as if to say duh.

"Listen, you're not Doogie Howser."

"Who?"

"You don't know who Doogie Howser is? Look it up on Google. I don't want you diagnosing yourself. Something serious could happen."

"I don't want you worrying about me all the time."

Although conflict mediation was my specialty, I was at a loss for a solution to this problem. How do you stop a boy from worrying about his mama, and how do you get a mama to stop worrying about her boy?

"Do you want me to leave you two alone, ma'am?" the nurse asked, filling the vacant space in our dialogue.

"No. Could you please speed it up, so I can take my boy home?" I replied to the nurse before directing my attention back to my baby boy. Small pieces of lint and dust had decided to assemble in his hair, most likely after he hit the ground. I plucked and pulled each piece in an attempt to make the time go by faster and shift my focus while he attempted to smack my hand away.

"Stop it, Ma. I'm not a baby."

"You will always be my baby." I bowed and kissed his forehead a few times. "You're my number one priority."

Mason met us at our stoop and scooped Nate up like he was Superman. "I've got it from here," he whispered over his shoulder to me. All too grateful for the opportunity to take a breather, I didn't voice my concerns. I hopped into the shower and let the droplets of water slap my face. Mason walked in and out of the bathroom freely to brush his teeth, use the toilet, and ask me if I would be much longer.

"I might be... would you like to join me?" I offered. The potential to be close and to share the contents of our hearts were what we needed right now.

"Kira, do you think now is the time for that?"

Thank God he couldn't see me rolling my eyes as he scolded me. My mind wasn't even as close to the gutter as he thought it was. At that moment I wanted comfort and to find it at home.

The bedroom was empty by the time I finished showering. I kneeled at the foot of our queen sized bed and began my customary evening prayers.

"Thank You Lord, for my home, son, and husband. Thank You for my health and wealth. Amen." There wasn't a pressing need for two hours of prayer in my life anymore. Working in HR had taught me not to spend my energy on resources that proved to be fruitless. Long, extensive prayers were fruitless. Not one of my prayers had been answered. Nate was still sick, and based on Mason's dry reception to my offer to join me in the shower, our marriage was as anemic as our son.

Chapter 9

After two days of bed rest, unlimited ice cream sundaes, and tons of fluids, Nate decided he'd spent enough time at home and was ready to return to school. By six o'clock in the morning on Friday he was in his school's white polo shirt and navy sweater vest that bared the gold logo of Emblem Academy.

I shuffled out of bed and attempted to make as little noise as possible. My outfit had to be changed three times. After wearing lounge pants for forty-eight hours, nothing fit right. Adjusting the collar on the gray blazer with pink leather piping, I evaluated my fourth outfit of the morning.

"Ma, you look fine," Nate said, pressing his dome into the meaty part of my shoulder.

"You sure?" I reevaluated my reflection. I'd taken my weave out during our two days at home. My roots needed to be touched up and my curling iron wasn't small enough to catch my cropped cut. I had settled for a comb out slicked back with pomade. As I fingered my short hair, I thought of Quincy's offer. If I recorded with him, I could get a tutor for Nate, he could stay home when he felt ill, and go to school whenever he was up to it.

"Let's go, Ma. You really do look fine," he declared before marching out to get his things.

The commute from our home to Nate's school and then to my job were event free. There wasn't a Quincy McAdams spotting nor a police investigation or sick passenger to slow things down. My only prayer was that the rest of the day would go as smoothly.

Once I settled in at work. I asked Meena to hold my calls and limit my visitors to emergencies only while she typed up my notes for Jeffrey Henson's case. It seemed simple to me. A round of he-said-she-said gone wrong, mixed with a few dangerously low cut blouses which led to the inappropriate jesting and flirting. An early morning visit to the marketing and sales department revealed there was no need for the usual hardcore investigations and interviews I typically conducted. First of all, both the women and men in marketing and sales were equally crass. They seemed to do nothing but encourage each other with curses and offensive jokes. Secondly, the water cooler was still the place to find out the best gossip. It seems there was some information little miss Diona left out of her sexual harassment complaint. A course in sensitivity training and appropriate workplace communi- cations would go a long way for the entire department.

I recommended that Henson should be sent to sensitivity training first, and then he could spearhead training the rest of the department to redeem himself from the sexual harassment allegations. I turned on iHeart Radio and clicked on the MacMusic station I'd created after bumping into Quincy.

The sultry and soulful sound that marked his brand of music flooded the air. I clicked Send on my computer to send the report, relaxed in my chair, and indulged in the fantastical life I would live working alongside Quincy at MacMusic. Visions of the music we were going to make didn't fill my thoughts. The tours and all-nighters in the studio dominating my time popped up once or twice. What did appear in a majority of my machinations were visions of Quincy's straight white teeth, the curvature of his lips, and the sparkle in his eyes just before he kissed me. Many more of those would quickly become a part of the music making process for us, I thought as heat gathered in my body. I slid my arms out of my blazer and closed my laptop cutting my inappropriate thoughts short. Right on time, too. Meena knocked on my door and announced that Greg Keegan, the VP of HR, needed to see me.

"Let him in, please, Meena."

Greg walked in with his usual artificial smile plastered on his face and planted himself in front of my desk. "Kira, on the departmental level you're one of the most devoted employees. You rarely take time off." He opened the button on his mustard yellow blazer and rested one hand on his hip. "I understand that before last week you only used two sick days in about three years, but it has been brought to my attention that you've taken a few days off in just this week alone."

"Mr. Keegan, my son has Sickle Cell Anemia."

"Call me Greg, please." He smiled

"Greg, do you know what that is?"

"It's a terrible disease that affects the African-American community in daunting proportions." He informed me, still grinning like a court jester.

"Yes, it is. I've been taking days off to care for him." That may not have accounted for the time spent with Quincy, but it was the main reason. "Is there a problem with that? I hope not because that time is protected by the Family Medical Leave Act."

"That's fine," he intoned, trying to placate me. "But, because of your distractions, I think it's best I bring in Robert Daniels to consult with you on this case. I believe that—"

Maybe Onyjie was correct; I needed the Lord because the devil was at my door and a demon sure nuff was whispering in my ear, *smack the hair plugs off of him.* I cut him off and said, "Excuse me." I frowned so hard I could feel the muscles in my face tighten. My cold stare must have been too much for Greg to bear. He backed up and cleared his throat before he attempted to stab me in the back again.

"I know that you are usually very thorough. You're the best we have at conflict resolution. We've had the lowest turnover rate since you've been spearheading the HR department. But it has been brought to my attention that there was an eyewitness to Diona's complaint whom you did not interview."

Jesus, help me not to bust this man in the face. This visit was purely part of the ridiculous game he was playing. Greg has been in my office about three times since I took over this department four years ago and now he wants to question my work ethic. I stood up just to make sure he understood I would not tolerate anyone interfering with my work regardless of how distracted I may appear.

"It's also been brought to my attention that you've been screwing Diona for the last three months."

Greg's mouth popped open like a can of Coca Cola. His face and neck turned just as red as the can. "You must have thought it was some secret. I work in HR and know everything going on in this building, including the hidden things. I also know that the only reason you're standing in my office is because you and Mr. Henson wants to see whose urine has the strongest stench." I pointed at him. "I will not allow you to use my office to determine the winner."

"Now, you listen, Mrs. Seagram," Greg snapped back. "I know people in this building, you don't have to continue on as the director of HR. Your workload can be reduced until your son gets better and that wouldn't violate your rights, now would it?" He smiled. His green eyes were aglow with revenge. At that moment he must've felt like he was standing on the summit of Mount Everest and I was a rock broken off during his ascent. "Now you play nice with Robert. Listen to his insight, and I'll see to it that a donation is made to Cure Sickle Cell Foundation. I might even get someone to approve Cloud Nine helping you with those hefty medical bills," he said before strolling out as if we'd just had lunch.

This wild onslaught had to be punishment for the kiss I exchanged with Quincy. *Nah, God isn't that petty.* "Are you? I know I haven't been praying much, but I'm asking for a little intercession over here, if you're listening. Amen."

I flopped into my chair and flipped open my laptop. The little mail icon was blinking on my email account. Quincy was the sender and 'Beats for Your Record' was in the subject line. I closed the tab on my email to focus on my new task of rereading the statements Diona submitted accusing Henson of sexual harassment, followed by the statement Henson submitted in his defense when he realized the accusations made against him. I'd taken few notes during my observatory visit to marketing. Now it was all making sense. Diona was sleeping with Henson, who thought that since he's now the VP of sales and marketing he could say what he wanted to his ex-woman with no backlash. Just like a man; he was wrong because her new man is the VP of HR and he has no qualms about fighting dirty. I folded over and collapsed onto my keyboard.

I didn't sleep with anybody and I was the one getting dirty.

After rereading the statements, I had to retract my report from the system. My focus was on stringing my words together into a tightly woven tale that would force Robert Daniels to see things the way I did instead of him trying to retrain my eyes. At the exact moment I placed my fingers on the home row of my laptop's keyboard, Onyjie came bursting through my door like a streak of illegal fireworks on the fourth of July.

"Is you crazy?" She paused and flicked her new Indian Remy weave over her shoulder. "You have that man making donations to the American Sickle Cell Anemia Association on behalf of your son. Or, should I say you and Mason's son. Is you crazy?"

I folded my hands across my chest and repeated her question "Is you crazy?"

"I know what I said. Is… you… crazy? You better pray to God that Mason doesn't find out about this. Right now it's only on MediaTakeOut. Let's touch and agree that the coverage of this stops right there," Onyjie offered, extending her hand towards me.

"That is the last thing I have to worry about." I reclined in my chair dismissing her offer to ride on the coattails of her faith to prevent the decomposition of my marriage. I rubbed my bare feet along the carpet. The feel of the carpet was soothing. "What would Mason be doing looking at MediaTakeOut?"

Onyjie shrugged her shoulders and asked, "Who doesn't look at MediaTakeOut?"

"Generally, people with jobs. You're worried about me, Onyjie, and you're spending your time trolling social media sites." I sucked my teeth. "Are you trying to get fired?" I asked.

"Are you trying to get divorced, Kira? This whole situation is ridiculous," she piped. Onyjie's sharp tone of voice served as the antecedent of any sermon she was about to deliver. I drew my chair in close to my desk and glued my eyes to my computer screen. My fingers flew up and down the keyboard inserting sentences that were more suggestive —to help Robert see things my way. However, they didn't reveal my true recommendations. Diona needs to wear blouses that can actually be buttoned or be removed from the department. I couldn't add any of that so I recommended that her work area be moved so she'd feel more comfortable.

Regardless of the clack of my keyboard, Minister Onyjie continued with her sermon. Instead of clacking, I pounded on the keys hoping the noise would be a deterrent.

It was not. She was determined to save me and my marriage.

Onyjie opened her mouth wider, stepped closer to my desk, and shouted, "When was the last time you went to church?"

I clicked on the calendar tab on my screen and counted the Sundays.

First Sunday I was away at a retreat. On the second and third Sunday I was in the ER with Nate whose blood levels had dropped so drastically that he couldn't walk on his own. By the fourth Sunday, my body and brain were so steeped in stress that getting out of bed was a more daunting task than washing the windows. It had literally been a month of Sundays, but I wasn't about to let her beat me into a coma with that information.

"It may have been awhile since I was there, but my name is on the prayer list. My church family knows what I am going through and they've been praying my strength in the Lord. Okay?"

Onyjie sat in one of the upholstered chairs in front of my desk. She crossed her legs and rolled her shoulders. "Don't you think Samson's mother was praying for him after all the turmoil he was in? All of Israel was probably praying for him? But you know what?" She swatted her new hair off her shoulder. "He didn't get his strength back until he asked for it himself. Girl, at some point you have to ask God for eyes to see and the strength to do His will and not what ya want."

"Preaching piety is easy when your faith isn't being tested," I retorted.

"Kira, it seems to me you haven't been studying for the test. Your faith has been riding in the backseat for a long time now. All that's left is your family. Don't screw up what you and Mason have," she pleaded like she'd have to choose who she wanted to live with if there was a divorce.

Onyjie had been spoon-fed Bible verses since she could eat solids. She'd grown up hoping and praying that she would marry a man like Mason. All I wanted was to marry a man that was my friend. All I wanted was to experience passion and comfort. All I wanted was everything I'd never seen. My mother had been the submissive wife at my father's beck and call, but I never saw him give himself up for her. Onyjie didn't know what that had done to me and she would never understand that. It's hard to curse a person out when you know they mean well, but since I hadn't been to church in a month I could hear a good cursing fit welling up inside of me.

Before I could get the first one out, my phone rang. Apparently, God was concerned about one of us and He intervened before it got ugly. Silence blanketed the room. Onyjie's eyelids dropped low and zoomed in on my office phone like the scope of a sniper's gun. I placed my hand on the phone and tapped the receiver with one finger taunting her. A pained expression took up residency on her usually soft, angled face.

"Are you going to answer the phone?" she asked on the fourth ring.

"Hello, this is Kira Seagram speaking."

"Is it him?" Onyjie mouthed over the table, "Is it?"

"Excuse me." I raised my hand to silence Onyjie and focus on what was being said. "Please, repeat that?" I requested, dropping my voice to a soft coo as if I was asking a baby to go to bed.

"Foreclosure... I don't understand... back taxes." The more Mr. Steven Henry of Manhattan Credit Union went into detail the less I understood. I scribbled his name and number down on a Post-it and tried to read it back to him, but I couldn't. A thick coating of water covered my eyes. The image of me sleeping on a cot, with Nate struggling to fall asleep as I hugged him close to my chest, made it extremely difficult to concentrate.

The more he spoke, the faster my strength depleted. My hand quivered under the weight of this news causing the phone to fall from my fingers.

I hadn't asked Mason for much. Keep my bed warm and a roof over my head. Maybe the distance he'd created between us, the coldness, and the hardness that had enveloped our bed was preparation for the streets we'd be sleeping on. The first set of tears broke through and slid down my cheek.

Chapter 10

Onyjie may have detested my behavior and attitude where Quincy was concerned, but that didn't prevent her from coming to my aid. She scooped the phone up as it fell from my hands like a running back taking the ball from the quarterback.

"Hi, Mrs. Seagram was called away from her desk. I will remind her to call you back upon her return." She placed the phone on its base. "Kira," she whispered, allowing all the pretense to leave her voice.

I didn't have the words to explain it to her.

It was too much for me to believe. In one week Nate was hospitalized because of leg ulcers, The VP of HR was coming for me, and now I was about to be evicted.

There was only one comforting thing that came to my mind as I tried to figure out how to resolve this conflict—making music with Quincy McAdams of MacMusic.

Maybe it was time to call him.

"What can I do to help?" Onyjie inquired, interrupting my thought process.

I pressed my hands against my temples to quash the bulging and pounding I felt going on in my head. My brain seemed to be expanding. "Nothing." I sniffed. "There's not a darn thing you can do," I stated, banging my fist on the top of my desk. "Just leave me alone for a while. I've got to take care of my business."

"I don't know what's going on, but please don't do anything drastic," Onyjie requested before retreating out of my office door.

I pinched the corners of my eyes closest to my nose to stifle my tears that were running out like this was the 400 meter dash at the Olympics. I pressed my body into the back of my chair. It tilted back just enough for me catch a snippet of the city skyline from the window behind my desk. The corner office signifies your arrival in the business world and I could see why. I had two expansive windows that overlooked Manhattan—one in the center of the office and one window positioned right behind my desk. There was something about the sight of the cool and pointed antennas that littered the periwinkle sky that calmed me. Just that small glimpse of the city behind me assuaged my anger. My focus returned, and I went back to revising my recommendation for Diona's sexual harassment charges.

By the time I pressed Send on my computer, spatterings of violet filled the sky and clusters of people were speeding up and down 42nd Street. My cell phone vibrated in my bag. Mason had called me three times and Quincy had sent me a text message.

`Shifted some things just to record you sing`

`Meet me in the studio Monday @ 9`

The screen on my phone lit up as another call from Mason came through. I pressed decline opting to save my rant for the privacy of our home and not the sidewalk. There were two sights I couldn't stand to see on a city sidewalk—a woman in run over heels or a woman screaming into her cell phone sharing all of her problems with Manhattan.

All of the lights were off in my house—or soon to be former abode—except for a flicker of light escaping from the dining room. The only time we ate in the dining room was during the holidays or when my mother-in-law popped up for a surprise inspection. I made my way to the dining room, praying not to hear my mother-in-law's voice. She could be described as sweet, but something was always going on in her life that required us to dole out at least a thousand dollars to solve her problems. That was probably why we were behind on our property taxes, I assumed as I rounded the corner.

"Welcome home, Mrs. Seagram," Mason said, waving his arm over the spread he had laid out. The flicker that caught my eye came from the small, rounded Chinese lanterns he'd hung from the ceiling and the tea light candles that he'd lined the window boxes with. The titillating scent of my favorite pork stew wafted through the air.

Mason took light and graceful steps toward me. He stripped my purse from my shoulder and flung it in the corner. Next he undid the buttons on my jacket.

"What is all of this?" I asked, taking note of the ambiance he'd created and even the effort he'd put into his own appearance. His locs were freshly twisted and his beard was no longer as bushy as a cypress tree. It was trimmed and manicured. I noticed things about him I hadn't seen in a long time like his sculpted cheekbones, his long and tender eyelashes, and charming mouth that seemed to have been drawn with one stroke of a paint- brush. "What's going on, Mase?" I asked again after spotting the sparkling white grape cider and cheesecake at the center of the table.

"It's a celebration," he declared, kissing me. "Come on." He scooped up my hand to lead me to the table. A plate of pork stew over rice and peas was waiting for me.

"Sit down and dig in; we have a lot to cover." Mason took my coat from me. "My lady," he said, pulling out my seat.

I eased into my seat while Mason stepped out to hang up my coat. Wonder took bites of my mind. I didn't know what he had to celebrate, but I knew it had to be big. While pork stew was my favorite, he was more of a "no pork on my fork" kind of brother. Say what you want about me, but I was in Bible study the night we went over Acts and the Lord told Peter, call nothing he created common or unclean. I don't mind pork on my fork or bacon with my breakfast. Unable to resist the chunks of meat floating in a pool of gravy, I picked up my spoon.

"You started without me," he squawked as I stuffed a heap of stew into my mouth. My head bobbed up and down. The flavors popped. Cilantro and basil tiptoed on my tongue, and the meat was so soft, there was almost no need for me to masticate.

"So, what's the special occasion?" I asked as the meat melted like snow in my mouth. This would not be enough to make up for our home being in foreclosure, but it was enough to delay my impending wrath.

Taking a seat beside me, Mason laid his hand over mine. "Let's pray before we talk." He bowed his head and cupped my hand tightly. "Dear Heavenly Father, I thank You for how You have blessed this union. I pray that Your love will continue to reign in this home. Bless this food, in Jesus' name."

Mason drew my hand to his lips and kissed the back. "We're set to record our song for the Songs of Zion contest this Monday and they want to film us during recording as part of the promo materials for the contest."

"Monday?" I asked, sulking. The same day that Quincy wanted to record with me. "So, are we definitely going to win this?"

Mason paused before answering me to withdraw a folded sheet of paper from his back pocket. "If you sing this."

"If... you're celebrating an if?"

"It's not an if. God gave me a vision."

"I hope it was a vision of someone paying the back taxes on this house."

His heart must have stopped when I said that. His mouth flapped open and his eyes latched on to mine. "Yes, your secret is out. The bank contacted me today. At work," I balked. "And I'm sure that they called you as well."

"I don't want to discuss that right now. We're celebrating God and His great plan for deliverance," he said, filling his plate with stew from the bowl on the table.

"Deliverance. Our son has leg ulcers, our home is about to enter foreclosure." The events of this week had to be weakening my tear ducts. I couldn't control them from moment to moment. His honest eyes met mine, and the tears shot out like water from a fire hydrant.

"We need a real solution," I demanded from him, banging my fist on the table.

"Don't ruin this," he warned, cutting his eyes at me. "The realest solution I have for you—for me—for us is prayer. The Lord has brought us this far. Now we just need to exercise a little faith," he stated, holding up his fingers like he was measuring salt.

"Will one gospel competition pay our back taxes? That's all I want to know, Mason." I huffed. At this point I was beyond frustrated and his colossal-sized faith had corroded my appetite. Christians like Mason were beyond my level of comprehension. Them unshakable ones that could praise their way through any series of unfortunate events that life flung at them really messed me up. I mean I could do the whole not lying, not coveting, and I'd already passed up on committing several murders on the job. This thing with Quincy was borderline adultery, but so far I hadn't bitten on the bait, but this faith stuff was more than I could do.

"I know this isn't what we planned, but trust me this is what He has prepared us for and He has more prepared for us on the other side of this."

"Does He have some money prepared for Nate's medical bills?" My coverage wasn't bad, but we still had out of pocket cost and the way things were looking in my office today, if Jeffrey Henson didn't get fired, Greg was probably going to make sure that I was.

Mason grabbed my hands and held them tightly in his palms. "I feel just as powerless as you do. My son is wasting away before my eyes. I can see the pink meat under his skin." He clamped down on my hands tighter. His palms had become moist. "All I can do is pray and call on my Father. All I can do is hope that His unfailing love and tender mercy will show up soon." His usually strong voice betrayed him. The bass hid in his belly and his words wavered as they walked out of his mouth. Mason's eyes bulged out of the socket. I'd seen this kind of posturing before. He was fighting back tears. This was the face he'd put on when he'd stood by his mother's side holding her back from jumping into the grave as his father's body was being lowered.

"Kira, just trust me. And if you feel like you can't trust me, then trust God."

I pointed at the ceiling and then at him. "Why should I trust y'all, when y'all the ones that got me into this situation?"

"And who do you think will get us out of it?" Mason said before departing from the dinner table and retreating to his prayer room.

Chapter 11

"Quincy McAdams will save this family," almost came out my mouth, but I'm not a blasphemer. When it comes to saving, I know only Jesus' name belonged in that sentence, but Quincy could help with our monetary problem. Money didn't seem to be a problem for him. I could get an advance from MacMusic for songwriting credits and take care of this family. That night I dreamed our home was no longer in foreclosure. I was about to sign the deed to the townhouse on the hill of Saint Nicholas Avenue I'd been eyeing for a while.

Monday arrived and the house was still on high alert. Mason wasn't speaking to me out of affinity for His God, and I was beyond trying to please him or coax him into pleasing me.

I jumped into an ordinary black suit as if I were going to work and doubled back after dropping Nate off at school to change my clothes. From the footage I'd seen of Beyoncé in the studio, it seemed like she always had on layered t-shirts and joggers while recording. To mimic her relaxed style, I threw on a sheer white tank top over a blank tank with a pair of boyfriend jeans and nude pumps. I topped the look off with layered gold chains. After skipping down the hall to check myself out in the full length mirror, I felt confident about my look and sure of my abilities. I phoned Quincy to confirm our studio time and ask him if he'd pay the back taxes on my family's home. The idea sounded ridiculous in my head, but I would figure out a way to ask with couth.

"KK, I hope you're not calling to cancel on me," he said immediately abandoning all formalities.

"Of course not, Q." I giggled into the phone. "I was calling to confirm that we're still on."

"If you're ready to make some hits, baby, so am I," he whispered.

"Beyond ready," I said hesitantly. I didn't want him to get comfortable calling me baby. As the director of human resources, I knew how this would play out. "Listen, I wrote some songs, too. I'm ready for this," I added to keep the conversation flowing. Making Quincy pump his brakes before I got the green light would be career suicide. Besides, I enjoyed the back and forth. "I also wanted to ask you something."

"Anything you want, you got it," he moaned into the phone

I laughed. "You don't even know what I want."

"All right, baby girl, give me a few minutes and I'll swing by to pick you up and you can tell me all of your demands. I didn't expect any diva requests this early."

"Nooo…" I replied quickly. "I'm not trying to be a diva and to prove it you don't have to go through the trouble of picking me up." I gathered my lyrics and stuffed then into a folder. "I can make it there on my own."

"Listen, every MacMusic artist rides around in style. That Mazda might be all the rage with the moms at Emblem Academy, but the music biz is totally different. Besides, you look good in my Range."

"Quincy, you are always exaggerating. I haven't even released a single, let alone a hit record. My Mazda will do just fine." I laughed.

"KK, let me come and scoop you up. Please allow me to relish in every opportunity I get to spend time with you. Don't worry about the hits. All I do is make hits. We will have a hit right out the gate."

"Do you really believe that?"

Silence was his response.

"Quincy," I yelled.

"Why are you yelling at me, woman?"

"Because you didn't answer me. Did you hear what I asked you?"

"Trust me; you'll be pushing your own Range in a minute. I believe in you so much that I ran to the garage. That's why I didn't answer you right away. I'll be at your house in a minute," he said and ended the call leaving me staring at the screen of my Android.

With the announcement of his impending arrival, I added a deep burgundy felt hat, diamond studs, and I slathered on brown lipstick that made my skin glow. To avoid looking like I spent the morning playing in my mother's makeup, I skipped the blush and eye shadow. I opted for a coating of mascara and lined my lower lids with kohl eyeliner to make my eyes pop.

Quincy's Range Rover rolled up in front of my stoop at the same moment that I stepped out of my door. I tottered to the car and hopped into the passenger side. We inched through side streets at the speed of a turtle.

"You must miss Harlem," I joked. "As slow as you're going."

"What if I missed you?" Quincy grinned as he turned down a side street. "Could you imagine rolling through this block come spring and hearing one of your songs bumping from that window?" He pointed at a townhouse with chipped paint and a lean to it. Regardless of the condition of the exterior anyone could tell that house was the spot to stop at if you wanted to know what was new and hot in Harlem. The fall winds were rolling through, along with a slight drop in the temperature, but the windows of this house were wide open, bathing the streets in bass and the up-tempo beat of the latest Nicki Minaj record.

"Let me hear one of them songs," he commanded while we were stopped at a red light.

"Now?"

"Yes, now."

I shuffled through all the songs I'd been working on since I bumped into Quincy. "How did this get here?"

"What is it, babe?" he asked, taking his eyes off the road and pinning them on me.

"Nothing," I said, stuffing Mason's song into the middle of the pile.

"Come on now, KK. I'm ready to hear something." He reclined in his seat holding the steering wheel with one hand and casually placing his other arm on the armrest. "Give it to me, baby." He reached up with his free hand and tapped his ear.

"I want to be free to show you me. Give me your hand and let me show you what your eyes can't see. Let me be free. Let be free. Let me be freee."

Quincy raised his hand to stop me. The cars before us lurched up an inch and we remained stationary. "Is your husband prepared to be married to a bonafide R&B diva?"

My eyes turned from his crisp profile to the trees that could be seen through the passenger window. "Mason doesn't know."

"What doesn't he know?"

"He doesn't know anything that's going on right now."

"He doesn't know your recording, or doesn't know about us?" he asked, squeezing my leg.

"Us," I replied, looking Quincy in the eye. There was something daunting and salacious about the way he said 'us'.

"Didn't you want to ask me something?" he asked, covering my hand with his. My eyes walked up his tone arm and gazed into his dark brown eyes. He parted his warm, peach lips and licked his bottom before repeating his questions.

My gut told me, don't take the bait.

The passion and the purpose for my existence seemed like they had collided. I wasn't even getting top billing at work anymore. My home was about to enter into foreclosure; maybe this really was my moment even if the circumstances aren't right.

"Ummm…" I exhaled a sharp breath and looked at my lap. I didn't want to see his expression when I asked this. Just then we stopped at a light and he lifted his free hand from mine, traced my jawline with one of his fingers, and tilted my face towards his.

"I've been a lot of things in the past, KK, but I am serious about this. Whatever you need I got you."

With that I blurted out my request "I was wondering how soon I'd get my advance. I need $28,598.32."

"Money, that's all you want?" Quincy threw his head back and laughed at my request while stepping on the accelerator. "That's lightweight. I got you, but how about this. I've never given an artist an advance without a contract and all that. You know how bad that would be for business?" He glanced at me for a moment. "Here's what we will do. We will record the song you sung and you'll join me at this showcase I'm supposed to be hosting at The Spot in Soho on Thursday. I'll put your name on the list. If you rock house, I'll give you thirty grand and then some."

"You know how I do things when I'm on stage," I replied.

"You better bring it."

"Q, I'm going to give you the best that I have." I stared at his profile waiting for his response.

Quincy did something dangerous and took his eyes of the road to meet my gaze. "Kira, don't open the door to a room I can't enter." His words and his eyes were so sharp, they sheared the fibers of my heart. I hadn't thought about how things would play out beyond this moment, beyond the music. Daydreams were one scenario, but now my dreams were alive. It was too late to turn back now and even if I wanted to, I realized it was too late as we rolled onto the Westside Highway.

I shimmied into a sheer spaghetti strapped black dress that embraced every curve of my body.

"Where are you running off to?" Mason asked as I slipped my feet into a pair of black pumps. "You've been on the go all week."

Thank goodness he didn't ask where I was all week because my nerves were rattled just trying to come up with a lie that covered my tail tonight. I didn't have any good stories prepared to explain the entire week.

"Business event at Lounge XYZ. There's currently a sexual harassment case under review at Cloud Nine, so they want me around to prevent any other cases."

Mason walked up behind me, clenched my waist on both sides, and drew me into him. "You look like a sexual harassment case waiting to happen." He bent over and grazed my exposed shoulder with his lips. "Let me be the first."

"Mason, not now." I slapped his hands and dipped out of his reach. The three quarter lie I conjured up was burning the lips of my soul like a spoonful of sriracha sauce. My goal was to tell as much of the truth as possible so I didn't have to tell a full-fledged lie. The business event line was true, maybe not Cloud Nine business, but business nonetheless, and I was reviewing a sexual harassment case. I thought I'd made it out of his reach, but Mason grabbed me and pulled me into him again. He dotted my neck with kisses. "Something is off. There's distance in the air."

I spun around to face him. Mason wouldn't believe what I was saying if I wasn't looking him in the eyes, and the delicate curve of his eyelashes accentuated the light in his large, brown eyes. They demanded honesty that I wasn't ready to give. "Everything is fine," I said and shrugged.

"Is the foreclosure thing still bothering you?"

"No. Everything will work out just fine."

Mason leaned in and kissed my forehead, the tip of my nose, and then my lips. He pecked and pecked until my lips melted under the heat of his desire. One of Mason's hands travelled up my back until he reached the nape of my neck. With his fingers he massaged and stroked my head, running his fingers in and out of my hair. I don't know what he was trying to do, but with each stroke my body became more pliable in his hands. Parts of me that had ached and long to connect with my husband did.

"Stay," Mason whispered into my ear. The hairs of his beard tickled my skin causing me to giggle and fold into him.

"I can't…"

"What if I won't let you go?" he asked before picking me up and carrying me to our queen sized bed. He dropped me into the folds of the champagne comforter laid across the bed.

"Mason, what are you doing?"

"What I wanted to do the other night," he stated while kissing my chest.

"Mase, I have to go," I insisted as the whir from my phone vibrating on the dresser filled the room.

"Stay," he whispered again drawing my arm to his mouth. He stroked my wrist with his lips. "Please stay."

Desire and exasperation gathered and decorated his eyes with a subtle dimness. What he had to be frustrated about was beyond my understanding. I'd never once asked him to tear up his dreams, open his palm, let the wind carry them away, and call it faith. I'd never blown cool air on the flames burning inside of him. Somehow his dreams were large enough to fill him and still fit into the church walls. The more I allowed myself to think about what I would have to give up tonight my body grew tense under him.

"Kira, I don't know what you want from me." Mason let my arm slip out of his hand. "What matters to you more, what's going on out in the world or here at home?"

I sat up in the bed and used my elbows to support me. I tried to ignore his six-pack, the small stripe of hair that went from his navel to boxers, and everything else about him that was screaming *I am a man please take me as I am*. "Mase, I could ask you the same thing. You're always on your knees with your head in the clouds. God is in control of heaven, He doesn't need your help up there, but I can't make you understand that, can I?"

I didn't wait for his response. It was likely to be a mixture of scriptures on being a good wife and the importance of prayer. I drew one leg up at a time from beneath the arc his open leg stance made over me, grabbed my clutch and my keys, and darted out of the house. In the end Mason would thank me for being so resourceful.

The fluorescent lights that created an evening rainbow along

Broadway flooded my car and kept me company on the drive downtown. Whenever I found myself at a stop light or trailing behind someone who was taking the new twenty-five mile an hour speed limit too seriously I did a vocal exercise to warm up for tonight's set. It had been a long time since I'd sung anything other than the hand clapping and foot stomping inducing gospel melodies Mason crafted for the praise and worship portion of devotion at New Vision. If the sweat that lined my palms as I gripped the steering wheel were indicative of how well I'd do tonight, I was going to drown. In the parking lot near the lounge I adjusted the windshield mirror and gave myself a good talking to.

"Future. Foreclosure. The sunshine is waiting on you to make a move. Sing yourself silly tonight, girl. I give you permission to live a little." I refreshed the fuchsia lipstick that decorated my pout and floated across the cobblestone streets of Soho towards the entrance of The Spot.

Quincy must have pulled a few strings to get into this lounge nestled in the back of the Trump hotel. A warm and sensuous vibe encircled me, lithe and sprightly bodies adorned the chocolate leather couches. The gold Chinese lanterns casted a ripe orange light that made everything look fresh and desirable under the dark glow. I tucked myself away against the stone wall near the DJ booth in the corner and scanned the crowd for Quincy's shiny, bald head. Just like wind in a sail, he caught my eye and skirted through the crowd of bodies to get to me.

"What took you so long?"

"Hi, Quincy. I'm glad to see you again. No, I had no trouble getting here. Thank you for asking."

Quincy wiped his whole face down, took a full breath before responding. "I'm sorry. I was getting nervous."

"Why?"

"I thought you weren't going to show up." He stepped in front of me and planted both of his hands on the low wall behind me hemming me in. "I thought you changed your mind about us… I mean working with me."

I cleared my throat and focused my eyes on his soft velvet navy loafers with gold trim accents. He matched the decor of the place. Once again I could feel a spike in blood pressure and small surges of electricity went off in myriad places in my body. I was tempted to touch him, kiss his lips that were now poked out. "I haven't changed my mind about working with you, but where exactly is this performance supposed to take place?" There wasn't a stage that I could see, so I had to ask. "I'm not dancing on the bar. If that's what you had planned, you can forget it."

A sly grinned cropped up, and he grabbed both of my hands. "You will perform right in the center of the room and you better tear this place down. You understand?" he said, raising my chin so that our gazes met.

I nodded in agreement and he dragged me over to the DJ booth. "DJ Turk, this is the new girl I told you about. Drop that track I gave you and give me a mic."

The DJ handed him a mic, and Quincy took off into the center of the room bopping to the beat of the track.

"It might be Thursday, but we're getting ready to turn up in here. For those of you who don't know me, I'm Q the CEO of MacMusic and I want to introduce y'all to Kira Love. Tonight she's going to do a little something for y'all. I want y'all to tell me if I need to keep her in the studio or unleash the beast. Do you think y'all can handle that?"

The crowd roared a unanimous yes. Quincy looked back over his shoulder at me and thrust the microphone in my direction.

I jumped on the mic and did a run. *"Freeee, freee. I want to be free to show you me. Give me your hand."* I stuck my hand out in front of a patron with sparkling blue eyes and a Crest smile. He latched on and jumped up to dance with me as I continued cutting up the song. I mixed jazz runs over the pounding bass and dance rhythm. The rest of the crowd bought into the routine. Women kicked off their pumps and jostled around on top of the couches to dance, and the more reserved surrounded us on the dance floor until the beat faded out.

"How am I doing guys?"

"Kira! Kira! Kira!" they chanted.

I could not wait until Quincy wrote that check for me.

Chapter 12

The knobs on the console used in the studio glistened, greeting us upon our arrival at the studio. I ran my fingers along the bottom row sliding each knob up and down like a zipper. Hovering behind me, Quincy pressed his body into mine. My insides burned faster than synthetic hair. The weight of his body reminded me of how long it had been since Mason had even attempted to be intimate with me. Two weeks. I did the electric slide to the right before I allowed myself to languish in whatever this was that I was feeling.

Nostalgic.

Neglected.

Either way, it was a bad mix—especially in an empty studio.

"You better get used to having me around," Quincy said as his eyes danced all around my body, inviting me to get into trouble with him.

"I don't know if I can... I shouldn't..." My words warbled out of me.

Quincy took a large step into my personal space again. This time we were chest to chest. He lifted my chin with the tips of his fingers to meet his eyes.

"You can and you should." He cupped my face like he was cradling a porcelain bowl. His hands traced the lines of my neck, my shoulder, and arms until he reached my hands. Our fingers merged, pulling me in closer to him. "I'm not going anywhere and you, my dear, are not going anywhere either," he stated as he withdrew a check from his back pocket.

Pitching a tent was a bad idea. All I wanted to do was record a song and get that advance money, but here he was looking better than bacon and grits. Hints of sandalwood catapulted off of his skin and lodged in my nostrils. Again I found myself tempted to touch him. Tempted to discard my morals and my wedding vows, but bless the Lord, I wouldn't have to make that decision today. The red light positioned above the studio door flashed, indicating that someone wanted to join in this session.

Quincy broke our grasp, stuffed the check back into his pocket and pulled out his cell phone. "I hope Raoul remembered to inform that new artist we wouldn't be recording today," he mumbled. He shifted through his messages and stared at the screen of his phone for a while.

"I'll be right back." Quincy rested his cell phone on the boards and ran out of the studio.

Quincy's flirtations and my advance had increased my heart rate. Finding myself alone, I did a breathing exercise to get my mind and vocals together. However, I couldn't get the two in sync with the constant murmur that Quincy's phone made as it vibrated. The disturbance drew my eyes to the screen.

Do not get caught up & don't get yourself into any trouble

Trouble? Caught? Was I signed up for a Death Row Redux? I shook my head and tried to remind myself that this was Quincy. Nerdy college chemistry tutor Quincy McAdams. It couldn't be that bad.

Don't get CAUGHT UP flashed across the screen of his phone again. Now, curiosity may have killed the cat, but I would not let ignorance be the death of me either. Contrary to proper etiquette, I picked up Quincy's phone. I tried punching in the important numbers I remembered from Quincy's life; fortunately for me, he was still self-centered. The phone unlocked on the first try as soon as I punched in 0621—his birthday.

I scrolled through messages from Raoul, his studio engineer until I hit the exchange that was the catalyst for these warnings.

Finally, I understood what my pastor meant when she prayed for the veil to be removed from the eyes of her people. The temptation that drew me to him and the desperation that blinded me had fled. Now anger was gnawing at my bones. I collected the few things I'd come with and prepared myself to ask for forgiveness. No longer would I be seeking absolution for adultery. I'd need to find a suitable penance for a homicide because when I was done with Quincy McAdams someone would have to call in a 1-8-7.

"Sorry about—" he began as he glided through the door interrupting my plot to avenge myself.

"So, this whole, 'let me produce your album, I'm not going anywhere' wasn't about me?" I asked, shaking his phone from left to right. I looked at the screen and read Quincy the text messages he sent to Raoul. *"We need Kira's voice. We're in the red and even though Diamonique's album was a success with the critics, the fans didn't buy it. With Kira's milky voice flowing over one of my rock hard beats, the fourth quarter is sealed.*

"I don't know how I let you fool me again," I said, stomping my foot.

"I can explain."

"I didn't ask you to explain. You can take your explanation and…" I flung the cell phone at his head. Either I was bad at throwing or he had good reflexes. The massive rectangular chunk of metal just grazed his temple and crashed into the wall.

"You're taking those words out of context. This industry isn't easy to survive in. It's a lonely place. Do you know how hard it is for me to find someone that calls me by my first name? Or be embraced and wanted by a person, not a weave wearing thot looking for a come up, or somebody with their hand stuck out? Kira, you're not walking out on me again," he declared, tightening his jaw.

The more he spoke, the easier it became for me to recognize his lies. "I don't have to listen to this. I don't know what kind of games you're playing, but it seems like the very thing you don't want people to do to you was what you planned on doing to me," I shouted. "The devil is a liar."

Quincy threw his hands in the air. "So, now you're all high and holy since I'm not prince charming anymore."

His words cut into me. The knight I'd designated to rescue me was using his lancet to impale me. "Just a few minutes ago you were standing right there," he pointed at the space in front of the boards, "ready to sin with me. Where was your morality when you were breathing hard and staring all in my face?"

This time I stared at him. I could see myself in his eyes. Their emptiness seared my flesh. I wanted to cry out to God, but I felt like a young girl who'd soiled her dress before getting her picture taken on picture day. There wasn't a good enough justification to excuse that kind of indiscretion. I took a step backward and attempted to walk around him. With one wild swing he latched onto my arm and pulled me in close to him.

"Yes, my company is in trouble. Yes, I wanted to use you to bring it back, but that's not the only thing I wanted to revive. I want that old thing back, and you do too. I see it in your eyes," he asserted, stroking my cheek with his free hand.

"Correction, you saw it in my eyes," I said, attempting to twist out of his grip, but the more I wriggled the tighter he held onto me.

"KK, I'm so lonely. I want to be with someone who *knows me.*" Quincy bowed his head and his strong shoulders slumped down.

"I do, too," I replied. "You keep on calling me KK, but my name is Kira. Quincy, you don't know me... now, you know who I was. You may have seen something in my eyes, but look again." Quincy raised his head an inch. Our eyes met and locked. I tried to use my eyes to whisper into the ear of his soul. He'd burned more than a bridge with me. It was more like an entire city was scorched by the fire of this farce. Quincy released me but remained in my path.

"Are you going to get out of the way?"

"Do you think it's that easy?" He snarled, reaching for me.

I sucked in a deep breath to pull myself up and jumped behind the rolling chair positioned in front of the boards. The chair became my physical shield, but in my heart I prayed for my true shield to come and help me. "Please cover me with Your feathers, Lord. Let your truth be my shield and buckler," I said, mouthing a verse from Psalm 91.

For the first time in weeks I could hear and see clearly. The beauty that adorned Quincy's face faded away. The face of a gargoyle stared back at me. The eyes that hypnotized me now were bulging and frightened me. His poised and perfect feathered lips now dripped with saliva and his desire to suck the life out of me was now as transparent as plastic wrap.

The truth of the scripture, the devil comes to steal, kill, and destroy, couldn't be more evident. His presence in my life wasn't the divine intervention I thought it was, but a distraction sent to steal my gift, kill my relationship with God, and destroy every relationship I had in my life. There was no way I was going to just give up everything now that I could see what was going on. As foolish as I felt hiding behind a chair, I prayed for God to just help me find a way to escape, and He did.

I withdrew my cell phone.

"What are you doing?" he shouted.

"Calling 911. Can you imagine the headlines? 'MacMusic turns into a Mad House' or 'MacMusic CEO Holds Woman Hostage in Studio'. Trust me, people will know your name then." I didn't blink, but stood firm in my resolve and waved my cell phone at him. "Please, just let me go. I've got to get back to where I belong."

Quincy snatched the rolling chair from in front of me and threw it across the studio. It banged against the Plexiglas that separated the booth and the boards. He stepped in front of me, his chest heaved up and down, and the heat of his anger singed my skin.

My words, as simple as they were, demolished the blockade that separated us, yet it created a new monster for me to conquer. Though fear made all the blood in my body pulsate faster than the Rocky River, I tried to hide it.

"If you walk out of that door, don't come back—"

"Come back? To you? For what? Quincy, you've got nothing for me."

"You'll be back." Quincy nodded then tapped the pocket he'd tucked my check into earlier. "Women like you always come back."

"The devil is a liar," I shot back over my shoulder as I shuffled past Quincy. "And let's be clear about something." We turned to face each other. "You better not say one word to my son, either, or else I will most definitely be speaking to the media." I cautioned him by snapping a photo of his face before walking away for what I hoped would be the last time.

Chapter 13

I stumbled through the doors of the studio and hit the pavement hard with each hurried step I took. My quick steps morphed into a sprint to the train station. I ran faster than a gazelle on the African plains with a pride of lions after her, albeit, a little less graceful. I caused a collision on every block I trampled through. I left a dog walker tangled up in leashes and two nannies rattled after a failed attempt of running around their charges. I hopped on the C train and hoped it would carry me to the church fast enough to catch Mason and the choir before they left for the studio.

Before Mason went to bed I heard him tell George, the drummer, they were all going to meet at the church to pray with the pastor before heading into the studio. I took the lyrics for Mason's song out and rehearsed them while I rocked from side to side on the platform.

As I stood there, I felt like one of the five foolish vir- gins Pastor talked about often. I had not prepared for this day and now all I could hope for was an abundance of mercy to fall.

The church doors were open and Pastor Stone was there handing out tracts to passersby.

"Praise the Lord, Sister Seagram," she said, wrapping me up in a warm embrace. "It's been so long since I've seen you," she added after releasing me. "You must be so excited about the progress the choir has made. This is a real blessing."

I lowered my eyes to escape the accusations her words carried even if it was unintentional.

"It might be hard to accept this blessing right now," Pastor Stone rubbed my shoulder, "while caring for a sick child, but trust me, the Lord has got that precious family of yours in the palm of his hand and is upholding you."

All of the words I had prepared in my heart disappeared.

"As glad as I am to see you. What are you doing here?" Pastor Stone asked when I didn't respond to her initial greeting. Her question and sweet burst of faith rocked me.

Suddenly the heaviness of my absence from the presence of Lord and self-imposed exile from the household of faith choked me. My guilty conscience crippled me. I hadn't been much of a wife, a Christian, a mother, or anything else. I no longer knew why I was there. Inadequate wouldn't be an accurate adjective to describe how I felt standing before Pastor Stone. So much was wrong in my life, but I'd never taken the time to seek any wise and godly counsel. Onyjie had been my only confidant. Because Mason served on a ministry board, I never confided in anyone at the church to maintain our privacy and protect his image as a man of God.

"Daughter, what's the matter?" Pastor Stone asked in the tender voice she used on Sunday when it was time for the benediction.

Something inside of me told me to keep quiet and move along, but my better sense told me that there was no reason for me to be struggling with my faith. My husband ushers three thousand people into the presence of God and seemed to be able to bring Jesus down from the third heaven when the praise was low. I shouldn't have this many problems.

"Let's go and talk inside," Pastor Stone suggested possibly because she'd picked up on my uneasiness.

"Thank you, Pastor Stone, but I just came here to catch up with Mason," I said finally deciding to reject this opportunity to clear the air. Mason didn't even know what was going on. I figured now was the least opportune time to confess my sins.

"Well," Pastor Stone rolled up the sleeve of her plaid blazer, "Mason went back home to pick up the song lyrics he left behind. He said something about changing the song because you weren't here. Now that his problem is solved that leaves us with plenty of time to chat. Come inside."

The usher who was working the door with Pastor Stone stepped up and took the tracts from her hands. I followed her inside to her office located in the back corner of the first floor of the church. A few pictures of Pastor Stone with a variety of city officials lined the wall behind the desk and a photo of her with the congregation at her first pastoral anniversary sat in the center.

I plopped into the cushion of the cream chair parallel to the desk and buried my head in my lap.

After I shed a few tears, Pastor Stone interrupted my pity party. "Pick your head up, daughter," she said, stuffing a Kleenex between my fingers. "Don't waste tears weeping over yourself when you have the gift of salvation. Weep for those unsaved folks who don't know Jesus. Let's pray about your situation. Tears never changed a thing, but prayer will turn things around like a boomerang."

I raised my head from my lap and dabbed at my tears. "Pastor Stone, this entire month has been a catastrophe. My actions haven't help things. Basically, I haven't been acting like a child of the Kingdom."

"I will tell you again, hold that head up, Kira." Pastor Stone used her index to raise my chin. "Hebrews 4:16 tells us to come boldly unto the throne of grace, that we may obtain mercy, and find grace to help in the time of need. We should be ashamed of our sin, but not so ashamed that we can't admit that we have sinned. Or else there's no room for God's grace to come in."

"Mason and I have been having a rough time lately with Nate's illness and I...I..." My voice trailed off. Thank God Pastor Stone picked up where I left off.

"And you've been looking at the grass on the other side of the fence."

"Dang." I snapped my fingers. "How did you know, Pastor?"

"I'm a woman too, made of flesh and blood just like you." She extended her forearm and pinched her skin. "Now you try it, Kira," she said, offering me the opportunity to pinch her.

"I believe you," I said, smiling.

"Then I hope you'll believe this—temptation is not a sin. Jesus was led into the wilderness to be tempted in Matthew four verse four, but He saw through every temptation proving how mighty the Spirit of God is. So, don't beat yourself up for being tempted."

A sense of relief washed over me, but it didn't last long as Pastor Stone continued.

"Now what you have to do is reconcile what's in your heart with who you are and where you are with Christ before it turns into sin. Jesus didn't give in because the things Satan presented him with didn't move Him. The only thing in His heart was pleasing the Father. What's in your heart, Kira?"

Exasperated, I sighed and slumped over the arm of the chair like a rag doll. My heart was filled with so many wants, needs, and desires that I didn't know what to name first, but I knew what I could not say. Pleasing God had fallen lower and lower on the list with each obstacle I faced. The realization of how weak and selfish I'd become besieged me and the tears flowed freely from my eyes.

"Don't cry, daughter." Pastor Stone patted my face with a Kleenex just grazing my skin like she was dusting a porcelain vase. "This is good for you. If you endure temptation, you shall be blessed."

"Pastor Stone, I don't feel blessed," I said.

"If you made it here, then you're on your way to the blessing. As you reach and fight through this temptation to fold up your faith you'll get that crown of life promised to us in James. What you need to do is talk to Mason about this and every other act that Satan is attempting to use to break you down. Let Mason pray for you and for your family."

"What?" I shouted, bolting upright in the chair. "I'm ashamed that God even knows what I had been planning. There's no way I can tell Mason. Do you know what would happen?"

"I'm not crazy," Pastor Stone said calmly, answering the one question in my head that I didn't say aloud. "I'm trying to teach you how to live by the Word. James 5:16 instructs us to confess our faults to each other and pray for each other and healing will occur. For 'the effectual fervent prayer of a righteous man availeth much'. Imagine how different things would have been if Bathsheba told Uriah how she was feeling."

"Solomon came from David and Bathsheba's union."

"He sure did, but their first child died because 'sin bringeth forth death' and in God's plan of supreme love He let the innocent baby die for David's sin, just like Jesus did for us. God didn't need David to sleep with Bathsheba in order for a wise man to be born. That was his mercy on David's life once he repented. Could you imagine what He would bring forth if you repented and worked on your relationship with Him and with Mason?"

I heard her, but I was having a hard time accepting what she was saying. Telling Mason what was going on sounded like a quick way to make an already complicated situation even messier.

"Pastor Stone, what time is it?" I asked, looking around her office for a clock.

"Ten after one," she replied still staring at the face of her gold watch.

"Mason should have been back by now. I'm going to the house and see if I can catch up with him. I thought showing up here might help us or help me, but I'm even more confused about what to do. I can't go on like this, I can't take care of my son, and I can't mediate situations at work with this clouded mind." After blurting out all of that, I rose from my seat.

"Let's pray before you go, sister." Pastor Stone extended both of her hands for me to hold.

I grabbed them both and closed my eyes.

"Lord, I come before Your presence with thanksgiving. Thank You for Your love, mercy, grace, and comforting spirit. Lord, I ask that You cover this marriage with the seal of Your love. Give Kira clarity in her mind's eye to see You. Purge her that she might hear from You, be able to take comfort in Your words, and see her husband for who he is. Help her to find strength in her times of weakness and not give in to temptation. Restore the joy to her life, in Jesus' name, Amen."

Chapter 14

It didn't take long for Pastor Stone's prayer to work. Reinvigorated and feeling full of hope, I pranced my way to the house. I hoped that someday I would be as strong in the Lord as our petite powerhouse preacher.

My quick steps ate up the never-ending Harlem blocks that spanned between 145th Street and Lenox Avenue to our home on 135th Street and Frederick Douglas Boulevard. Excitement swelled in my chest as I glimpsed the glittering rectangular blocks of cement that led to our house. It seemed as though God was really shining His lights on my home to lead me back to Him.

My quick gait morphed into a quick jog until I heard a hard crunch beneath my feet. What I thought was glitter and the glory of God guiding me was actually shards of broken glass. My eyes followed the trail of glass that stopped at Mason's body stretched out on the sidewalk.

There were only two choices present: rush to Mason side or call the cops. I chose the former and dropped to my knees. The blood leaking from his side coagulated and formed a thick, burgundy coating on the ground that resembled the disaster I caused when I spilled an entire bottle of Sally Hansen Red Wine nail polish. The sight of his blood squirting out of his chest reminded me of a line from one of Pastor Stone's sermons, 'we are but dust and one day we shall return to that dust to meet our maker.' I couldn't recall what verse or what book she said it could be found in, but I didn't want to testify to the truth of that scripture today.

Mason was ready to meet his maker. He was born ready I believe. Mason had to be sanctified from the womb the way he ran up and down the aisle of New Visions of Christ. He wasn't a backsliding sinner like me, Jesus was probably waiting to greet Mason, but I'd just had a revelation. I wasn't ready to give up my husband.

Imitating what every actor did when someone was wounded in a movie, I lifted his head into my lap with one hand and applied pressure to his wound with the other. Sirens roared in the distance and the hole in his side swallowed my hand.

"O Lord, send deliverance today. Send deliverance this way. O Lord, send deliverance. O Lord, I repent for what I've done. I regret what I've done. Send deliverance. Deliverance, O Lord." I sang over his body like I was fighting for a spot on "Sunday's Best." There's no way Mason knew when he penned those words that I'd be singing them over his body, begging for the angel of the death to pass over this house.

Bowed in supplication, my lips brushed against Mason's. The smooth ridges of his lips were dry and cold. His warm, chestnut brown skin was drying like parchment paper left out in the sun. I could still hear the sirens, but help had not come yet.

"Where am I?" Mason croaked, breaking up my two hour prayer fest. He squinted at me from his bed in the Emergency Room. "What's going on?" he asked, pulling on his hospital gown.

I rushed to his side and grabbed his hand. "You're in the hospital, Mase."

"Why?"

"We were hoping you could tell us. I found you on the sidewalk in front of my car, bleeding."

Mason patted his chest and worked his way down until his fingers arrived at his bandaged side. The corners of his mouth turned down, and he raised his head to look at me. Slowly, he brought his hand to his head and turned away from me. "I could have sworn that was a dream."

"No, that wasn't a dream. You have a concussion and the doctors said that you've lost quite a bit of blood. Mase, what happened?" I implored, plucking a piece of glass from his locs. "You were stabbed; you have to remember something."

He massaged his forehead with one hand before he recounted the details of his attack. "I went back to the house to get the music I'd written for Althea."

I glared at him. I had little right to be angry at the moment, but that did not lessen how much it disturbed me to hear that he had written a song readily available for the girl who only sang in a falsetto and wore low cut blouses to impress him.

"What?" He shrugged, misinterpreting my glare. I didn't bother to correct him.

"You were not there," he continued explaining. His words rolled out of his throat and sounded like dust. "I did what I had to do. When I walked out of the house there was a guy in front of your car so I rolled up on him." Mason balled his right hand into a fist and grinded it into his left. "He said, 'I don't want no problems' and I said, 'me either so just back up before I call the cops.' He said, 'Don't try to be no good Samaritan, dude, just keep it pushing.' Then he whipped out this long wire." Mason's eyes widened as he recounted the details of his attack as if his assailant was standing in front of him. "I said, that's my wife's car, and he lunged at me. We wrestled a little bit. I thought I had the jump on him until I felt a sharp pain in my side." He looked down at his wound and rubbed it.

"Thank God you're all right now." I traced his hairline with the tips of my finger. His locs were still slick and shiny. "Mase, that was the dumbest thing you've ever done," I said, whacking him on the shoulder. If I could have stabbed him myself, I would have for scaring me like that. "What would Nate and I have done without you?"

"Where is Nate?"

"Onyjie picked him up from school for me. She's still a little hurt that we didn't call her the last time he was hospitalized, so she was beyond thrilled to step in and take care of him. Do you want anything? Do you need anything? Do you want me to get the doctor?"

Mason shook his head and patted the side of the bed. "Let me get my thoughts together before they come in here and start messing with me. Kira, there's one thing I don't understand."

"What, Mase?"

"Why was your car parked in front of the house if you were at work? I thought you took the car. I would have used our car. I asked everyone to meet at the church, so I could get one of the church's vehicles to get some of the people in the choir downtown."

This was clearly the moment I was supposed to come clean. I studied him before responding. He was weak and still having problems focusing his eyes and it wasn't likely that he'd be able to attack me. Mason wasn't a violent man, but it didn't seem plausible to me that this moment would end with forgiveness and prayer if I told him the truth. He'd raised his voice at me three times in our ten years together, but this was new ground we were breaking. Reality was the nastiest tea to sip on and I was about to give him a full cup of it.

"Kira." He propped himself up on his elbows. "Answer me. Why was your car at home?" The warble in his words revealed his worry and the distrust that was bubbling in his gut.

I scanned the room for something that could serve as my focal point. I couldn't tell the truth and look at him. A cute still life of a fruit bowl hanging on the wall to the right of me held my attention.

"I…I…I didn't go to work—"

"But I thought that you were working on something so important that you couldn't—"

"Mason, just let me get this out."

He collapsed into the pillows behind him.

"I didn't go to work. I went to MacMusic studios in Chelsea to record a song. I…" I paused and took a deep breath and exhaled before getting deeper into my confession. "I used to date the CEO, Quincy, but-that-was-done-and-over-with-before-you," I blurted. "When I bumped into him at—"

"Nate's school," we both said in unison.

"Is that why he made a donation to Sickle Cell research? Have you been taking my son around that man?" Mason latched onto my wrist and gripped it so tightly that it began to burn. "Have you been sleeping with him?" He popped up and fell back just as quickly. He sucked his teeth, released my wrist, and clutched his side. "This is a bad time for you to decide that you want to confess your sins."

"Hear me out, please." I took my eyes off the dull orange in the painting and took in my husband's face. His jaw was clenched and his thick eyebrows were drawn together so tightly you'd think he had a unibrow. "Please, just listen to me," I pleaded. "I just need you to hear me."

"God, give me strength," he moaned, staring up at the ceiling.

"Don't start praying. Don't shut me out, Mason listen. First of all," I twisted my body to face him, "I didn't sleep with him." Mason pursed his lips together and twisted them to the side. "I went to the studio with him twice and he drove me home once."

"When?"

"Last week. That night I came home—"

"Drunk."

"I was going to say late, but I will admit I had a few drinks that night."

"You were drunk," he insisted, attempting to hoist himself up again. This time he used the guardrails for support. "Your eyes were all glassy and you were slurring your words a little. Is that who brought you the fruit basket?"

"Yes." I bowed my head in shame.

"You expect me, a red-blooded man, to believe that a man took you out for drinks, bought you a fruit basket, and offered to record a song featuring you out of the kindness of his heart, and nothing happened?"

Relief filled my heart when the doctor, flanked by two orderlies, opened the curtain and informed us that they'd found a room for

Mason. They wanted to keep him under observation for a little while due to his injuries and amount of blood he'd lost. I was grateful not to have to answer him right away, but that reprieve didn't last long. Seconds after the door to the room he'd been transferred to closed Mason began drilling me.

"Go on and tell me this fable. Nothing happened between you and Quincy MacAdams." He laughed a hard, disgusted grunt of displeasure.

"Nothing happened. He kissed me once, but I put him in his place and that was it."

"That was it. Huh?" He grabbed my arm and pressed his fingers so deep into my skin I thought he was a phlebotomist looking for a vein. "You want me to believe that? Do I look stupid to you? First you told me that fruit basket was someone else's. Then you told me you were at a company function the night you were with him. Today you told me you were going to work, but you made your way to the studio and met him instead of me. Why are you telling me this crap now? Isn't it enough that I got stabbed?" he asked, releasing my arm.

"I'm confessing because Pastor Stone said if I confess my faults to you that you could pray for me and I'd be healed. I'm scared, Mason. Am I alone in this?"

I'm not sure when I started crying. I didn't even realize until Mason used his thumb to wipe away my tears.

"Stop. Please," he said, interrupting me. "Come here." Mason patted a spot on the bed closer to him. He sucked his teeth when I didn't move. "Come here," he repeated and adjusted his body making room for me next to him.

I inched closer to his side. It was hard for me to get a read on him. His white teeth were still clenched together, but I didn't know if that was a grimace from a body racked with pain or a heart pierced by deceit.

"Come closer. Lay your head right here." He patted his chest and raised the sheet, inviting me into the bed. "Come to me. Let me do what I should have been doing—covering you in prayer instead of hiding behind it. I never wanted you to know I was weak. I didn't want you to know that I couldn't be your everything."

"I don't want you to be my everything. I don't need you to be my everything. Isn't that what we have the Lord for? What I need to know is that you are in this thing with me." I slinked into the bed and snuggled up beside him. My lips grazed his neck. The scent of myrrh and jasmine filled my nostrils. I dragged my lips over his skin again appraising his Adam's apple, his chin, and worked my way towards his lips.

"Let me pray before you take my breath away, Mrs. Seagram." He stretched his arm around me and drew my head in close to his chest. "Lord, I call upon You in the name of Your dear Son, Jesus Christ. Please Lord, look upon all the concerns of this family, knit our hearts together with Your cords of love so tightly that we desire nothing else. Help us to forsake our own desires and learn to put each other's needs before our own. Help me to forgive my wife and erase the thoughts of what I heard that Satan will try and use to divide this family. Lord, let Your spirit abide within us and cause our love to blossom until it can minister and heal, just as Your love did. Please, forgive each of us for being selfish and seeking our own way, in Jesus' name. Amen," he said, meeting my lips with a kiss. It started out soft and slow. As the fervency and the heat between us rose, I pulled back. "Are you allowed to do all of that with a concussion? You haven't been cleared for regular activity yet. Do you want me to get the doctor?"

"Not yet," he said. A smirk spread across his face. Mason bit down on his bottom lip then reached in and kissed me. His lips were soft and wet against mine. He dragged them down my neck and drew me in tightly. "I need to spend some time making sure you never allow another man to put his lips on you." He fumbled with the buttons of my blouse while looking up at me. "Let me remind you that I'm Mr. Seagram and you're Mrs. Seagram," he said before attacking me with a cannonade of kisses.

Chapter 15

The hospital released Mason after 24 hours. His blood transfusion went smoothly, and the doctors cleared him to come home. We rode home in silence; that transfusion had restored some of the brain cells that losing blood had depleted. All of the forgiveness and adoration had evaporated and it was back to being unhappily married.

"Don't you have any music to play?" Mason asked, crinkling his lips. The silence must have been making him itch as much as it was disturbing me.

"I don't have any Tamela Mann on my iPhone if that's what you're looking for," I replied before pressing the dashboard. "Play music," I commanded my smart car.

"As long as it's not MacMusic," he mumbled, turning his gaze away from me. He was hurting.

I inhaled sharply and tried to absorb that jab.

"We're almost home," I said. "There are enough walls up between the two of us. We've been provided this opportunity to break down the walls between us. Let's talk."

Mason's head snapped and all of his features folded into one wrinkle. "You mean I had to get stabbed while you were meeting your little boyfriend in order for you to tell me that there was something wrong. That doesn't sound like the work of the God I serve. Sounds more like the devil putting in overtime to destroy me and you know what the Word says…" Mason paused either for dramatic effect or for me to complete his sentence. When I didn't, he filled in the blank. "The Bible says, give no place to the devil. So, right now I'm not even going to discuss how you allowing him free rein in our marriage is my fault. Now, I'm going to ask you again: do you have any music?"

"I do, but your little diatribe was long enough to carry us to our front door."

Mason hobbled out of the car clutching his side. I offered to help him up the steps but he refused. A man's pride is a terrible thief. His silent treatment continued for the whole afternoon until Onyjie came by to drop off Nate. She worked the bell like she was cooking up a beat for the sequel to Drumline.

"That must be Onyjie," I announced.

"I'll get it," he said, inching out of his favorite seat. By the time he returned with the two of them in tow, Mason had dropped the Maggie Simpson act and his mouth was running faster than Al Sharpton's. "Pooka, look who finally came home and look at who decided to pay us a visit," he called to me, pointing at a giddy and smiling Nate and Onyjie trailing behind him.

"He's had plenty of candy and snacks so he ought to crash in a while," Onyjie stated as she entered the kitchen.

"Do you think you could make me a sandwich?" Mason asked.

"Turkey, avocado slices, and some relish, good?" I replied.

Mason rested his hand on the small of my back. "Add a drop of mayo and then I'll be out of you ladies hair," Mason added, kissing me on the cheek.

"Ohhh… girl," Onyjie groaned, pursing her full lips together after Mason left the kitchen. "You better act like you know and take care of that man."

"I'm going to tell you about that man in a minute. Let me get this sandwich together."

While I prepped Mason's sandwich, Onyjie entertained herself by playing Candy Crush on her cell phone. She didn't even notice I'd left the room to give him the sandwich until I sat down at the kitchen table beside her.

"Don't be running up on me like that while I'm playing this

game. Girl this level is timed," she said with a look of disgust on her face before laying her phone face down.

"I didn't know Candy Crush was such serious business."

"Well, now you know." She tossed her head, shaking her shining black Rapunzel ponytail. "Now, let's talk about that candy you've been crushing." She giggled.

"What are you talking about? I'm done with that whole Quincy thing," I whispered.

"I know. I can tell because that beady look in your eyes is gone," she said, pointing one of her decorated talons at me. "Your complexion looks better and Mason seems happy. I'm glad y'all figured it out. Let me know if you want me to take Quincy for the weekend."

"Slow down. We only seem to have things back together. I told Mason what happened between Quincy and me."

Onyjie shrieked and jumped back in her chair. "Why the heck would you do something like that?"

"I'm trying to serve the Lord now and I've got to be honest with my husband."

"And how's that working out for you?" Onyjie asked, crossing her legs and folding her arms in front of her chest.

"It's not." I sighed. "At first he was great about it. He was a little upset then he prayed for me and it seemed like things would be okay. We even made love in the hospital room, but now he's all cold towards me. The only reason he said anything to me right now is because you're here. He's barely spoken to me since we left the hospital."

"Don't worry, Kira," Onyjie said, resting her rounded fingers on her knee. "He's just getting over the initial shock of it, but you've got to do something quick before he retreats into that world of bitterness and contempt. It sounds like he's already at the borderline and you don't want him to become a permanent resident there."

"What am I supposed to do?" I huffed. "I'm already tired of

trying to crack Mason's shell to get past what's brewing in his head to become a part of his heart. Our marriage had become a convenient partnership, but we didn't begin like this."

"You have to do something drastic." Onyjie pointed at the scowl I donned whenever I had to step outside of my comfort zone. "Fix your face."

"What exactly do you mean by drastic?"

"I'm not sure, but if you want to fix this, do something that is drastic to get his attention. Just think of the lengths God was willing to go through to mediate the broken relationship between God and man."

I groaned. Although, I asked what she meant by drastic, I was hoping she meant cater to him, wear sexy clothing around the house, and fawn over him until that tough exterior corroded.

"Listen." She snapped her finger in front of my face to regain my attention. "God wasn't in the wrong. He didn't break up the relationship between us. We did with our actions. Our sins caused a separation between us and God and He still said, 'I love you this much.'" Onyjie extended both of her arms forming a cross. "'I love you so much I'm willing to send my son to die for you. I love you so much that my son will bear all of your shame and stretched out wide and high for all to see.' He did something so drastic to win back our love that people are still marveling at that sacrifice."

"You're still not telling me anything, Onyjie." I sucked my teeth at her and her holy aspirations. I hoped she'd find a husband just as holy or life would be hell for them. As I considered my own plight I realized Mason and I were both believers, but not to the same degree. "I can't die for him, Onyjie."

"But what can you sacrifice to show Mason that you love him and are committed to making this marriage work? How can you show how much you love him?"

The following morning I crept out of bed and knelt at the foot for a while. Prayer had been a thing of the past for me; since Mason's accident, I was trying to do it more often. There was one issue on my mind and that was how we were supposed to make it from here.

Drastic.

The word seemed to ride into the room on the back of the breeze coming in the window. It filled the room and danced around me.

Drastic.

"What do you want me to do, Lord?" I asked aloud.

I wish I could say that the Lord spoke to me in dreams and visions and filled my heart with assurance, but nothing of the sort happened. It was just me and the word drastic.

Nate sensed how off kilter things were in our household. He quietly got himself dressed without even badgering me about that hair of his and was waiting by the door when I got downstairs.

Drop off was simple. I didn't run into Quincy or his daughter while I was there. Once Mason and I start speaking again changing Nate's school would be one of the first items on the table for discussion. There was no way I could spend every morning ducking and dodging to hide from Quincy. It would be a selfish move considering it was my fault I now had to duck and dodge from him, but I'm sure Mason didn't want to show up for a PTA meeting and have to sit shoulder to shoulder with the man who was almost my lover.

When I rolled into my office, Meena was waiting to greet me with her American pie grin and a large cup of coffee in hand.

"Good morning, Mrs. Seagram. Your presence here was missed," she said, smiling while handing me my mug.

"Stop exaggerating." I fanned the air and inhaled the nutty fragrance emanating from my cup. "I only took off two days."

"This place hasn't been the same for those two days. If human resources is the glue that keeps a company together, you're the crazy glue that keeps the department together."

I smiled, nodded, and half listened as Meena recounted the various mishaps that had occurred in the two days I was gone. Maybe I should have taken a little more time off. Now that would be drastic, I mused. But I loved my job. At the office I'm the boss. I'm successful, and everyone worked their best to please me. It occurred to me then I'd been cheating on Mason way before Quincy popped up.

"Mrs. Seagram, are you all right?" Meena asked, interrupting my internal conversation. "It must be difficult for you having to return to work knowing that your husband was stabbed so close to home. You are so brave for coming back so soon after an attack like that. I think you should take it easy, but Mr. Keegan is not going to let you."

"Humph… I can handle him."

"Good because he's waiting for you in your office."

"Thank you for the heads up, Meena," I said and then strutted into my office. If Greg was looking for a battle this morning, I was certainly prepared to give him a fight. He wasn't about to bully the director of Human Resources into making a decision that would only serve one person's interests. That's not the way it worked. He was only concerned because the accused is his girlfriend's ex, otherwise he wouldn't be down here all involved in my affairs, and I was more than prepared to tell him that. Although I hadn't thought about his girlfriend's situation much while I was out, my mind had not changed.

"Good morning, Mr. Keegan," I chirped.

"Good morning, Kira. Remember, you can call me Greg."

"Mr. Keegan will do, seeing as you're not here for a social call." I rested my cup of coffee on my desk and removed my trench coat and scarf as if I were in the office alone.

"You're right, Kira, I'm not here for a little chat. I'm here to find out what kind of monkey business you're trying to pull running off for two days knowing you needed to finalize that report in the system."

"I did input my report into the system before I took off to take care of my husband who was stabbed during an attempted robbery. Is there a problem?" I smiled widely feigning ignorance to why he was so worked up.

"You know I specifically requested that you consult with Robert Daniels before completing that report," he said, meeting me in the center of the office cutting off my access to my desk.

Please Lord, don't let this man cause me to act a fool. At all times I try to remain professional and leave the hood at home, but Mr. Keegan had been pressing my buttons ever since he traipsed up in here trying to tell me how to do my job. My marriage is in shambles, the possibility for eviction is still looming over us, and now he wants to play with my job. I can't take too much more of this. I cleared my throat and adjusted my blouse before responding to him.

"I can recall your request as I am sure that you can recall my response. I typed the report and submitted it. I didn't expect to be out two days after that if you think I was trying to dodge you. I will not amend my report to support your shenanigans."

"If taking care of your husband is so important, then you should have remained at home because the next few days here will not be easy for you." He snarled before turning away from me and heading to the door.

"I don't know why I didn't think of that before." I clapped my hands together. "Thank you, Mr. Keegan, for the advice." I scurried to my desk and called Meena on the intercom system. "Meena, please print out the leave of absence forms."

I don't know what I'm doing, Lord. Please back me up on this.

Mr. Keegan stopped mid-stride and looked back at me. "What exactly are you doing?"

"Taking a leave of absence. After all, I am the director of Human Resources. I'll definitely approve this request. You're so right, my family is much more important than Cloud Nine and that will leave you and Robert with plenty of room and opportunity to make a mockery of this department without me in the way."

His jaw fell slack and his neck and face took on a tomato-red hue. "Are you serious? I know you love this job, Kira. I don't think you want to do something this drastic at a time like this."

There was that word 'drastic' again. This time it was being used to dissuade me from going home and that was confirmation for me that home was where I needed to be. My insides trembled a little at the thought of what would happen when I tried to return. When you work for a company that is run like a boys club, if they want you out, they'll get you out. Without this job there was no way we would make the mortgage or pay the back taxes on the house. On the other hand with this job there was no way we were going to make the marriage work. I was distracted. This place had become not only an escape, it had also become the scapegoat I used to cover up my tracks.

I left Keegan standing there with his mouth open while I called one of the executive officers and explained to him how my husband had been attacked, was still at home, and that we were both suffering from some mental anguish. He granted me permission to leave early and fax all of my documentation. I walked out with Keegan still standing in the doorway of my office.

My drive up the West Side Highway proved to be comforting and relaxing. The mixture of golden and auburn hues of the trees on the Hudson and the sheen of the fall sunshine sprinkled over the water gave me something to focus on every time I thought of Mason rejecting me.

"Please, Lord, let this drastic course of action be the anchor that stops this ship from sinking," I prayed as I dipped off the highway on 125th Street.

Chapter 16

The robust aroma of Frankincense greeted me at the door. I followed the scent up to the master bath. Through the curtain I gulped up Mason's almost perfect silhouette. My eyes wandered from his calves up to his firm quads. They weren't bulky; the muscles were neatly paved like a small side street. My eyes halted at his torso. He no longer had a complete six pack, but his abs were still smooth and sharp enough for my eyes to trace the lines in them.

I don't know why I was even remotely intrigued by Quincy. *Forgive me, Lord.*

He unraveled the make-shift knot he'd tied his locs into and shook his head from side to side under the stream of water flowing from the shower head. I stripped out of my work clothes and stepped into the shower with him. Mason shuddered as my body made contact with his.

"What are you doing?" he asked, looking at me from over his shoulder.

"Something drastic," I replied. "You know you still have blood in your hair?"

"That's why I wanted to wash it."

"Let me," I purred into his ear. I gathered his locs into my hand and ran my fingers through them. "Pass me the shampoo."

He reached up into the shower caddy and handed the shampoo to me. The bottle sputtered as I tried to squeeze some out. "Dip your head back a little."

"I don't know if I'm comfortable with this."

"Mase, you have to let me in. I'm your wife."

"You gave me some earth shattering news the other day. What do you expect me to do now?"

I didn't respond verbally. Instead I sunk my soap-filled palms into the middle of his hair and massaged his scalp. After a little kneading, he softened up like dough. The straight shoulders of his that I love, relaxed and fell.

"What am I going to do with you?" he moaned

"Love me," I pleaded.

"It's hard." Mason reached for one of my hands and placed it over his heart. "Do you feel that?"

The pitter-patter of his heart beat that was once as pronounced, rapid, and clumsy as a baby's first steps, was now a soft monotone.

"We have to do some groundwork and lay a brand new foundation." Mason let go of my hand. "Then we can build on it like the pyramids. But this is a good start."

"I think we need counseling," I said instead of good morning. He'd been home a month now and the first level of the pyramid we were supposed to be building had not been erected yet.

"What did you say, babe?" Mason asked, rolling over onto his back.

"I said, I think we need counseling, but I'd like to revise that statement. We need counseling." I ran my fingers through his prematurely gray chest hairs. I was glad he'd given up trying to get rid of them. They added flavor to his untamed look.

"I think we're doing just fine," he said, resting his hand on top of mine.

Things may have seemed fine to him, but I was about two days away from losing my mind. If Mason kept that behavior up, he and Nate would be visiting me in the psych ward of Harlem Hospital. The first month after Mason's attack was like living on an episode of Wipeout. One minute it seemed as though I was walking along the plank with ease, and then he'd snap and start questioning me or avoiding me. "We're not doing fine," I announced.

"We don't need counseling. Let's pray."

"I've been praying. You've been praying, and yes, things have gotten better between us, but there is still this distance between us."

"I'm sorry I can't just get over the fact that you were having an affair with another man," he said, flinging my hand from his chest. He rose from the bed. His sculpted torso and rounded biceps distracted me.

I slinked over to him and sat up in the bed in front of him. I pecked at the v his torso turned into.

"Sex will not make me forget, either," he said, taking a step back.

"I wish it would, then we wouldn't have to go to counseling."

"Who's taking me to school," Nate asked, busting into the room without knocking.

"Your father is. It's time for him to get back into the swing of things."

Mason arched his eyebrow at me.

"It is time, Mason," I said, looking up into his big round eyes. His eyelashes gently curled up and begged for my sympathy. "Go down to Boys in the Hood. The kids miss you and I'll meet you for lunch. Then we can head to New Visions together."

Mason rubbed his chin for a moment, then his fingers spread about and he raked through his beard. When he came to a conclusion he clapped his hands together and expelled a giant gust of air. "Here's what we're going to do." He pointed at Nate. "Finish getting ready and I'll meet you downstairs in about fifteen minutes and you…" He clasped his fingers together, drew them to his lips, and then pointed his interlocked fingers at me. "You call Onyjie and ask her to pick up Nate from school and I'll see you at New Visions this evening."

"This evening?"

"Yes, I'll talk to Pastor Stone and meet you there around seven." He pecked me on the forehead and threw on a crisp white t-shirt, loose-fitting Levis, and navy blue Pumas.

Alone with my thoughts, I opted to indulge in a writing session in my make-shift office as opposed to doing the laundry. It had been awhile since I'd stepped foot in there. The fiasco with Quincy had made me not want to so much as even think about singing, let alone call myself trying to write something. However, the emptiness that filled me compelled me to release it. After dusting the table off with a paper towel I sat down and scratched out some words. Maybe we'd be able to use the songs to feed us while we sang on the streets. During this time of restoration I thought it would be best not to bring up our pending eviction or our pending miracle, if you looked at it from Mason's perspective, but I don't think we could survive heartbreak and homelessness.

The time I spent in my hole whizzed by. I only had two songs to show for it and nothing on the dinner table when Onyjie and Nate pounded on my front door.

"Hi, my lovelies." I smiled.

"Hi, Ma. What's for dinner?" Nate asked while wrapping his arms around my waist. "I'm famished."

"Famished? Really?" I asked.

"Yes, famished, as in, starving. It's one of my vocabulary words and Mrs. Steinman says you can't acquire new words unless you use them regularly."

"Well, I'm famished too," Onyjie interjected, walking past us. "What's on the menu?" She sniffed the air. "I don't smell anything."

"Chinese or pizza. Y'all decide." I stuffed the money into Onyjie's hand. "I've got to run. Please behave yourself with your God Mommy, Nate."

"I always behave. She's the one you have to watch out for."

Onyjie and I fell over each other laughing. "I'm serious," Nate said in a very grown up fashion.

"Don't I know it, Nate. I love you. See you later," I said and blew a kiss in his direction.

"Have a good time," Nate offered before walking away.

Onyjie walked me to the door. "Please say a prayer for me tonight," I said almost begging. Her high rounded cheekbones rose as she smiled at my request. "Onyjie, pray that we get through this and get back to being in love."

"Listen," Onyjie said, resting her hand on my shoulder. "The only way love is going to become a part of your vocabulary is if you practice using it. No matter how he responds tonight *you* keep on pouring on the love. Love is patient, love is long-suffering yet still kind. That's God's love. Mason won't be able to resist you if you keep on bathing him in that."

Chapter 17

Mason was waiting for me at the door of New Visions. "Let's get this over with," he said through clenched teeth after kissing me on the cheek. He held the door open for me, but his posture was closed and tight. I think he was stabbing me with his eyes. It was hard to see his eyes through the dark tinted lenses of his sunglasses.

"It's so quiet," I said to Mason over my shoulder. The sanctuary was empty. I didn't even hear a sound coming from the classrooms that lined the back wall of the main sanctuary.

"Everything shutdowns here at six on Thursdays," Mason informed me. He rested one hand on my shoulder still marching behind me.

"Doesn't the Bible say something about God resisting the proud?"

"Now you're a scholar," he shot back.

There was plenty I could have said in response, but what good would that do. Mason still had my little escapade to hang over my head.

We filed into Pastor Stone's office.

"Hi Seagrams," Pastor Stone said with brightness in her voice. She hugged us and offered, "Take a seat on the couch or the chairs— wherever you're most comfortable."

We both dived into the couch. Mason sat down on one end and I took over the other.

"Are y'all saving a space for the angels, or is this the divide you were talking about, Sister Seagram?" Pastor Stone asked as she dragged a chair over to the couch.

"You already spoke with Pastor before speaking to me?" Mason asked, his face scrunched up into the knot of confusion.

"No, I've been speaking to you, Mason, and you're not responding so I called the woman of God."

"May I cut in here?" Pastor Stone asked.

Mason and I closed our mouths and directed our attention to Pastor Stone.

"Mason, why does it bother you that Kira contacted me?"

Mason nodded his head in agreement with Pastor Stone. "A man must be able to keep his house in order," he said firmly.

"Do you think by asking for help or counseling you're not?"

Mason paused and his mouth hung open for a moment. There was a response inside of him that was ready to come out, but he slipped his hand over his mouth and sat back. "This is hard," Mason mumbled without looking up.

"To keep things in order, they have to fall off the shelf and you do the necessary work to put them back where they belong. Abraham wasn't ashamed or hiding behind a façade when it was time to put Hagar out. And with all those servants and riches he had, you think people didn't know his business? Of course they did," Pastor Stone said, waving both her hands at Mason.

"This is a mess she created," he said, pointing his index finger at me. I think if Pastor Stone wasn't around he would have used the middle one as upset as he was. "She invited a type of Hagar into our household. Did she tell you that?"

If I had a super power it would be the ability to disappear. I didn't want to sit through Mason berating me.

"Another thing that Abraham didn't do was tell Sarah it was her fault. He turned to God to make sure he was doing the right thing, but he didn't say, 'Sarah we're having this problem because of you.' Abraham submitted himself to God and trusted that God knew what He was doing. Just like Christ, Abraham did the work that was necessary to cover up the errors that thinking with your flesh creates. That is the same call that He placed on the husband."

Mason's tender face scrunched up tighter than a slouch sock. "So, I'm supposed to just act like my wife didn't step out with another man."

"No, Mason, but you're supposed to forgive me," I sobbed. "You're always running around and singing about the God of a second chances. Doesn't that apply to me?" I scooted closer to him and rested my hand on top of his. "I didn't step out. We didn't have sex. I was tempted, but I didn't give in."

"She was planning a whole other life with him that I wasn't invited into," he said with his attention gaze pointed at Pastor Stone. He tugged at the neckline of his white t-shirt and sat up straight shaking my hand off his.

"And you've been living a whole 'nother life upstairs in your prayer closet and here at the church. Who does that leave me with?" Frustration joined us on the couch. I looked to him and he looked away. "Mason, I'm sorry."

"What does that mean?"

"It means you have to be ready to forgive now that she's ready to repent," Pastor Stone explained. She scooted to the edge of her seat and reached for the Bible that rested on one of the two end tables in front of the couch. Pastor Stone sat back in her chair and opened one button on her crème blazer before opening the Bible.

"This is your duty, Mason. Listen to what Ephesians chapter five, verses twenty-five to twenty-seven says. 'Husbands, love your wives, just as Christ also loved the church and gave Himself up for her, so that He might sanctify her, having cleansed her by the washing of water with the word, that He might present to Himself the church in all her glory, having no spot or wrinkle or any such thing; but that she would be holy and blameless.'"

Tears fell from Mason's eyelid's and splattered on his jeans as he mouthed the words of the verses along with Pastor Stone. I wished my spiritual I.Q. was up there. If it had been, a resolution could have come sooner.

"If she wasn't going to mess up, the word wouldn't be directing you to wash her with the water of the word. You know the water of the word that cleansing and refreshing feeling that comes after you've confessed your sins and you know that Jesus has taken them and buried them in the depths of the sea of forgetfulness."

Pastor Stone continued to work on Mason while I hummed the melody of "In the Depths of the Sea." Before I could stop myself, I was on my feet singing the hymn with my hands lifted in the air. I'd been waiting for the euphoria of forgiveness to take over me and the darkness that had taken up residency with me to move. It was happening now. Mason may not have been inclined to forgive me, but at that moment, I realized that God had forgiven me.

"Did you bring the car?" Mason asked when we walked out of New Visions of Christ. I shook my head. "I guess that means we're walking home," he said.

"That's fine with me," I responded, leaning into him. He wrapped his arm around me and we began our stroll home.

"Mason, if you never forgive me, I can live with that, but I don't think you will be able to."

"Do you remember when we first met?" Mason asked.

"Of course," I said, smiling up at him. Despite his short stature, Mason's full-bodied confidence always made me feel like he was towering above me. "That day changed my life."

"I can't remember it that clearly. What I do remember is how much I wanted to know you. I didn't know then that I would love you. I don't think I even considered that as a possibility, I just wanted to know you. And now that I do," Mason stopped walking and faced me, "you got me open and I can't just stop loving you." Mason slid both of his hands around my waist and pulled me into his body. "Do you think we could begin again?"

"I'm ready to begin again. The question is, are you?" I asked, pulling off his sunglasses, leaving him no room to hide the emotion in his eyes. They were wide and bursting with love. I could see that

I wasn't the only one who'd found freedom during our session with Pastor Stone.

"I'm ready," he stated, bending down on one knee. "Would you marry me? Again?"

I scooped his face up with my hands and pressed my lips into his. I pulled back and then pecked his lips a few times more. "Yes, Mason."

"Good, let's get married this weekend," he suggested, dusting the knee of his jeans off after he stood.

"This weekend? Where? Not in our foreclosed home." I folded my hands across my chest.

"I love the way your nose wrinkles when you're upset." Mason kissed the tip of my nose and continued. "In the backyard of our home. It's still ours and believe me, my God… our God will take care of that. The wedding doesn't have to be a big thing. We can get any minister who's available at New Visions to perform the ceremony. It will be our opportunity to bury both of our sins."

"Can I have at least two weeks?" I locked arms with him and tried to keep pace with his quick steps. "I need at least two weeks to get a decent dress."

"I'll give you two weeks on one condition."

"What?"

"You come to church with me on Sunday. If we're going to do this together then we have to walk this faith walk together."

I sighed and agreed. I wasn't ready to return and explain my absence or what had transpired between Mason and me to the congregants who claimed they cared, but were just looking for some information to discuss.

The first few Sundays back in the house of the Lord I felt awkward and ashamed. Mason had to drag me in a few times by reminding me that just like we expect God to be faithful He's looking for the same thing from us. I thought that everyone could see my sin. Pastor Stone explained that was a trick of the enemy to keep me out of the house of God and tempt me some more. Once that became clear I let go of my fears, clamped down on my faith, and my third row seat tighter than a one-cent coupon for composition notebooks during back-to-school shopping. I was more than ready to give myself back to God and to my husband.

Fourteen days wasn't a lot of time to get ready for a wedding. However, God knows what you need. Onyjie lived up to the meaning of her name and proved to be a gift from God. That woman trekked up and down the isle of Manhattan with me and a few days alone, helping me gather hibiscus and crocus for the decoration. The morning of the wedding, my eyes were still burning from the fumes of the glue gun and staying up several hours to create bejeweled bouquets for Onyjie and myself. A do it yourself wedding might be the cheap alternative, but it was a whole lot of work. Mason's idea to renew our vows was a good idea at the wrong time, but since there wasn't enough money in our savings to save the house, I decided not to fight with him and just follow my husband's lead. A little dip wouldn't hurt. I fanned my eyes in front of the mirror over my dresser and reminded myself that in a few more hours my greatest mistake was about to turn into a blessing, a new chapter. The plan in my mind was to indulge in this feeling, but Onyjie and her wedding 911 crew busted into my bedroom and put my plans on hold.

"Here." She placed a mug filled with coffee in front of me and two egg whites. I twisted my mouth to the side and looked at her. "Don't be ungrateful, girl, there are still children starving in Africa." Everyone chuckled at Onyjie's use of every mother's favorite line when their child refuses to eat what is set before them. "You're lucky you got that. If you even gain one ounce within the next few minutes you will not be walking down the aisle in this." She paused and drew a grey garment bag from behind her back.

"Is that the dress?"

"Yes," she squealed, unzipping the bag. I fingered the jeweled bodice and everyone ohhed and ahhed while we peeled the dress out of the bag.

"Jonathan, get on the hair, and Carla please set up the makeup station. My hair is already done, so you can start on my makeup. This wedding is scheduled to begin at one and it can't happen a minute later."

"Oh, my God I can't believe this. This dress and hair and makeup." I was so excited I couldn't swallow. "How on earth were you able to get a glam squad in here?" I asked.

"Onyjie does my taxes, and she never misses a beat. Girlfriend, here is fierce when it comes to the numbers," Jonathan said, snapping his fingers.

"Same here," Carla, the caramel beauty, added laying out her makeup brushes.

"I want the same honey glow you have, Carla," I declared

"Don't worry, I got you," she said, winking at me.

I scarfed down the two egg whites and took one long sip of my coffee. "Make me over," I commanded, clapping my hands.

I spent the remainder of the morning with my eyes closed, my head tilted back as the dream team, Carla and Johnathan, went to work on me. "Are you ready to see yourself, Mrs. Seagram?" Jonathan asked, whispering in my ear.

"Yes, I am," I said.

Then just as Jonathan was about to spin me around Mason's powerful voice boomed on the other side of the door. "Babe, can I come in? I need my cufflinks."

"Cufflinks," Onyjie scoffed. "Brother, the jig is up. We know you're trying to get in here and take a sneak peek. Beat it. It's not happening. It's a quarter to one; you can make it a few more minutes."

"Onyjie, quit playing. Let me see my wife," Mason begged on the other side of the door.

Onyjie marched to the door and cracked it. "In your patience possess ye your soul, brother. She's in good hands. Trust me, it will be worth the wait." She slammed the door in his face and joined Jonathan, Carla, and me at the mirror. "When I grow up I want to be just like you," she joked, pinching my arm.

"May I look now?" All three of them backed up giving me space to turn around.

I inhaled and placed both of my hands against my peachy cheeks in disbelief.

"Jonathan," I gasped, fingering my short hair that stood straight up and traced the purple hibiscus petals he weaved into my hair.

"You don't like it?" Jonathan asked.

"I love it."

The flowers complimented the eggshell color of the dress and seemed to make the beaded bodice shine even more. I ran my hands along the sides of the dress where it hugged my waist.

"You see why I said you couldn't gain an ounce," Onyjie added.

I nodded, admiring the excellent construction of the fishtailed dress. "Thank you, Onyjie." I grabbed her and hugged her. "I don't know how you got this dress in so little time, but I thank you."

"Don't ask and I won't tell," she replied, smiling.

I let her go and looked up at the ceiling. "Thank you, Lord, for this glorious day," I shouted then I turned to Carla. "Thank you, Carla for these smoky eyes."

"I tried to keep the color palette neutral since you have so much going on with your hair." She jabbed Johnathan in the ribs. "And your dress. You look fabulous."

We all squealed and clap our hands in delight like five year olds rummaging through their mother's closet when a soft rapt on the door interrupted our gush fest.

"Ma, are you ready to walk down the aisle?" Nate asked through the door.

I gathered the silky fabric of my dress in my hands and shuffled to the door to let him in. Since my parents weren't able to fly in from their vacation in Mexico, Nate offered to step in and walk me down the aisle.

He stepped in with his eyes beaming at me. "Wow, Ma."

"I could say the same thing, son. You're looking mighty fine in that tux," I said, fingering the sateen lapels on his black tuxedo jacket.

"I agree," he said, patting his 'fro. "My lady." He curled his arm and held it up.

I joined ranks with him and prepared to make my grand entrance.

"Wait a minute now," Onyjie said, adjusting the bustier on her one shoulder deep purple sarong like gown. "You're not going to compliment your God mother."

"Auntie Onyjie, you look great, but it is not your wedding and you're in the wrong position. You're supposed to march out before us."

I bowed and kissed him on his forehead. "I just love you, little boy." Again, I had to thank God for His grace.

Nate's eyes smiled back at me. Nate hadn't gone into a state of crisis since his last visit to the hospital and the leg ulcers, while they hadn't disappeared, the pain had subsided enough for him to participate in regular activities and walk me down the aisle.

"Step aside and let me get into position," Onyjie prompted us. She stepped in front of us before we could actually get out of her way.

"See you downstairs. You really make a beautiful bride," Jonathan said, snatching Carla's arm and dragging her out of the master bedroom.

"Let's make this thing happen," Onyjie said with a big grin on her face before starting the procession. She took slow and steady steps and led us to the backyard.

Onyjie threaded down the white strip of fabric that led from our back door to a large tree at the back of our small yard. Mason had begged me to cut it down when we first moved in. I refused. I thought it was a nice accent piece for our shabby little yard. Looking at Mason stand beneath it with his locs coifed and coiled into two barrel rolls looking so regal in the tailored gray tuxedo, I knew I had made the right call. The navy blue shirt he had on underneath made his big, brown eyes seem more illustrious than the day we met. I couldn't wait to get close to him and just smell him.

Odell, the saxophonist from New Visions, launched into a jazzy neo-soul version of "Here Comes the Bride" that had everyone swaying side to side. The small crowd that gathered to watch Mason and I renew our nuptials rose to their feet. Clicks, snaps, and flashes of cell phones accompanied Odell's playing.

When I reached Mason, even he was holding his cell phone up to take my picture. I batted his arm. "Put that away," I scolded him using my bouquet to cover my mouth and camouflage the chastisement.

"But you look captivating," he whispered, leaning in close.

Pastor Stone emerged from behind our great tree. "Is the couple prepared to reenter into holy matrimony?"

Both of us looked at each other and then at Pastor Stone and nodded.

"Everyone may now be seated," Pastor Stone announced. "Kira Seagram, do you—"

"Pastor, I've prepared my own vows."

"Kira, what are you doing?" Mason asked with a look of bewilderment in his eyes.

"If you'd permit me, I have something I want to say."

Mason cleared his throat. "Go ahead."

"Mason, when we exchanged vows the first time, we were entering into a contract with prearranged terms written by someone else for us to follow. Today we are entering into a covenant. I will love you with every fiber of my flesh. When you're not right I'll tell you that you are wrong. When it's dark, I'll be your light. I will follow you all the days of my life, creating a trail of love that will lead others to eternal life."

A tear roamed out of Mason's eye. He dabbed at it with the back of his hand. He wasn't the only one who'd grown misty-eyed after my declaration. From the corner of my eye I could see women digging in their clutches and purses for tissue and I could hear sniffles throughout the yard.

"I didn't prepare vows, but I'd like to say something."

My heart fluttered at the thought that Mason was willing to say something to me extemporaneously rather than praying on it or waiting for the spirit to provide him with words.

"Mason," I stretched my hand forward and rested it on his heart, "say what's in here."

"Kira Seagram, when you are weak, I will be strong. When you thirst, I will be your drink. I will fill your belly with love and the living water that is within me. I will be your provider and your protector until we depart from this earth. Through our love, the love the Father will no longer be a mystery because I will love you openly just as the Father has done for me."

A stream of tears departed from my eyelids. Mason stepped up and kissed each side of my face just below my eyelids.

I pulled back and used my bouquet to separate us. "What are you doing?" I asked, looking over at Pastor Stone, "She didn't say, you may now kiss the bride."

"Covenant not contract. I don't need someone to tell me when to honor my vows. I am going to be your comforter starting now."

Everyone rose to their feet and clapped.

"Based on that sound, I don't think there are any objections," Pastor Stone said, smiling. "I now pronounce you husband and wife. Mason, you may now kiss the bride."

Mason's hands gathered around my waist and he pulled me into his warm body. "Mrs. Seagram, I love you," he said before planting his lips onto mine. I let go of my bouquet and swung my arms around his neck and let my body fall into his embrace. We had forever to figure everything else out.

Chapter 18

Midday sunlight filled up my office at Cloud Nine and bounced off the top of my now bare desk. I surveyed the room I spent so much time in. After a month away it had turned into a foreign land. I never thought about what my last day would feel like. I didn't suspect it would be easy but nothing in me wanted to be there anymore. Things were going superbly well in the Seagram household.

"Girl, I can't believe you're leaving me here by myself," Onyjie said, bumping me with her hip. She joined me at the window. The majesty of midtown held our attention for a moment before she repeated, "I just can't believe it."

"Do you think if you repeat that enough times I won't go?" I laughed. "This won't be the first time you're here alone. Remember, you started a week before I did and I was out a month. That should have been enough time for you to make an adjustment."

"Yeah, but I didn't know you weren't coming back. You could have told me what was up," Onyjie said, folding her arms across her chest. Onyjie's dark chocolate skin usually shined in the sunlight, but her frustration darkened her complexion.

"I didn't plan this either. If this is the will of God for my life, I'm going to roll with it. I expected you'd be happy about this," I said, bumping her with my hip.

"Hate to bust up this farewell send off, but I need my wife," Mason chimed as he entered the office. He grabbed the last box from the floor. "We're double booked. We have to tape an interview at NY1 and we're doing Fox Five evening news today."

"All I know is I want front row tickets when you play Madison

Square Garden and don't be keeping my godson from me. She'll be down in a minute."

"Don't worry, we won't," Mason said before walking out.

Once Onyjie and I were alone again, I thanked her. I wanted her to know that we wouldn't be at this point if it were not for her. "Onyjie, I want to thank you for being a champion for my marriage even when I didn't want to be."

"Please, girl that's what friends are for," she said, swinging her freshly pressed twenty-eight inches of hair. "We all need someone to stop us from jumping in front of a train. Where's Quincy now? Filing for bankruptcy. It's nothing, girl."

I smiled. "I mean it. You hounded me and really impressed upon me that I needed the Lord actively involved in my life, not just on the nightstand. I mean if you had told me two months ago that I'd be recording with gospel legends like Seth Myers and The Sons of Jacob, I'd never have believed it." I had to press my hand to my chest to suppress the pounding of my heart. I was in utter amazement at how God had flipped this whole situation better than Hilary Farr flips homes on "Love It or List It." Mason's attack and subsequent overnight stay at the hospital kept the choir out of the studio and the producers of the competition selected another choir to take our spot. Despite the not being able to perform and participate in the Sounds of Zion contest, Johnny Upton, one of the judges and the owner of Divine Records, still offered the choir a three album deal with an advance that was large enough to pay the interest on our home and put a down payment on the townhouse I'd been eyeing.

"Ma," Nate called to me. "May I come in?"

"Of course, Nate."

"You better come and give your God mother a hug." Onyjie opened her arms wide like she was preparing to hug an elephant. Nate ran into them. His charcoal mesh sweatpants bounced with him. He crashed into her arms and rested his head against her chest.

"If anybody bothers you at this new school… What's the name of it?"

"Riverside Prep," he said.

"If anyone at Riverside Prep messes with you, tell them your God mother knows some goons."

"Cut that out," I said as I slung the straps of my cross body bag over my shoulder.

"I was talking about the mighty angels of God that encamp round about us." Onyjie winked at Nate and pinched his cheeks. "You keep on loving God and He'll keep on taking care of everything," she said, stretching out one arm for me to join in on the hug fest.

Accepting the invitation, I jumped into her arms and let them surround me in a circle of love. *This must be what it will feel like when I receive the overcomer's crown that Pastor Stone had told me about when I confided in her initially.*

"Don't worry girl, I will hold on." I kissed her on her forehead. "Now, I've got to go because you just inspired me to write a song. I love you, girl."

I sprinted out of the building dragging Nate behind me and into the car. "Hit the pedal and get me home quick," I commanded Mason while adjusting my seatbelt. "I've got a song in me and I want to sing it at service this Sunday."

For the first time since I'd been back, when I looked into the congregation from the pulpit I couldn't see the judgment.

"You ready?" Mason asked.

I nodded, and he beckoned me to come forward.

"Church, today my lovely wife is going to be singing a solo," he announced then handed me the microphone.

"Church," I said into the mic. "I want to encourage you this morning. Do you mind if I share a little testimony before I sing?"

"Go on, sister," someone shouted from the balcony.

"The song I'm going to sing today was inspired by a real trial—a real test. I thought that the battle was rooted in my flesh—nothing was going right and I lost sight of God. To escape my situation I tried to cover it up with another man. I was tempted to touch someone other than my husband, but God brought me through that trial. He saved my marriage and now I have to tell you that—*I am an overcomer. I am an overcomer. There's a crown reserved in heaven for me. Reserved for me. Though the journey may be long, my God is strong enough to uphold me. I am an overcomer. I am an overcomer. There's a crown reserved in heaven for me. Reserved for me. Through my problems, I'll praise him. Jesus is able—able to raise me up. Raise me above my circumstances. I am an overcomer. I am an overcomer. There's a crown reserved in heaven for me. Reserved for me. My God has written my name in victory. He clothed me in His righteousness in the face of the enemy. I am an overcomer. I am an overcomer."*

While I crooned out the words of the song, Mason directed the choir and together we triumphed over the enemy.

Discussion Questions

- In Chapter two Onyjie seemed very invested in Kira and Mason's marriage. Do you feel her interest was based on good intentions or was she too invested?

- Kira had a hard time giving up her dreams for Mason's plans. Do you think it's necessary for the wife to give up her desires to make a marriage work?

- Mason and Kira struggled a lot due to what seemed to be a spiritual mismatch. Is it possible for Christians to be in a relationship and be unequally yoked?

- How do you resist the temptation of committing adultery or fornicating?

- Why do you think Mason had a hard time acknowledging his role in the problems in their family?

* * *

Get your Inheritance in your inbox. Sign up for the Inheritance Books newsletter for updates on new releases, contests, events, and inspirational messages: http://eepurl.com/bkYUAH

Keep up with the Neophyte Author, Nigeria Lockley by signing up for the Nigeria Lockley Readers' Newsletter: http://eepurl.com/MFKH9

Other Titles by Nigeria Lockley

Seasoned with Grace

Sentenced to probation, thirty-year-old, supermodel Grace King must put her plans of transitioning into acting to extend the longevity of her career on hold. Desperate to keep a close eye on Grace and his job Grace's ambitious lawyer, Ethan Summerville, has her complete community service in the last place Grace wants to be—his church.

Instead of God, Grace finds a "chocolate drop" of a man— Brother Horace Brown. However, Horace isn't looking for a supermodel. He wants his woman saved and sanctified, but Grace has never met a man who has been able to resist her. Will Horace compromise his faith for a taste of fortune, fame, and Grace?

While Grace focuses on the pursuit of passion, Ethan finds one director willing to take a risk and cast Grace in his debut film, but this role fits Grace all too well. Will this film revive Grace's relationship with God and her career or bring her closer to destruction?

Born at Dawn

Thirty-four year old Cynthia Barclay knows that marriage is supposed to be for better or for worse. Unfortunately, for the last ten years of her marriage, Cynthia has experienced the worst that marriage has to offer at the hands of her abusive husband, Marvin Barclay. With the hope of saving herself and her family, she turns to the Lord. Expecting to see God manifest himself greatly in her life sooner than later Cynthia is not content just waiting. She wants out.

Abandoning her hope, her husband, and her two young sons,

Cynthia boards a bus from New York City to Richmond, Virginia. She begins a new life armed with six thousand dollars on a prepaid credit card, a sketchy plan for success, and a promise to return for her sons.

That is until she meets Cheo, a photojournalist with enough connections to take her where she wants to be and forget where she came from. After six years in Richmond Cynthia's dark past resurfaces. At the risk of losing it all—her past and her present—Cynthia returns home to right her wrongs. Has Cynthia chosen the right time to return home, or is it too late for God to restore everything she has broken?

About the Author

Nigeria Lockley possesses two master's degrees, one in English secondary education, which she utilizes as an educator with the New York City Department of Education. Her second master's degree is in creative writing. *Born at Dawn*, Nigeria's debut novel, received the 2015 Phillis Wheatley Award for First Fiction. Nigeria serves as the Vice President of Bridges Family Services, a not-for-profit organization that assists student parents interested in pursuing a degree in higher education. She is also the deaconess and clerk for her spiritual home, King of Kings and Lord of Lords Church of God. Nigeria is a New York native who resides in Harlem with her husband and two daughters. You can catch up with Nigeria online in the following places:

Website: www.nigerialockley.com

Facebook: www.facebook.com/authorNigeriaLockley

Twitter: www.twitter.com/NewNigeria

Instagram: www.instagram.com/NewNigeria